THE LONDON RECURRENCE

The Refusal of Time

Mark Anderson, PhD

Stability was never about control.

Copyright Page

Images are crafted using AI tools constructed by the author.

Mark Anderson, PhD
18 Dover Street Suite 492
Norwell, Massachusetts 02061

First edition
Printed in the United States

ISBN 979-8-9958085-7-2 (ebook)
ISBN 979-8-9958085-8-9 (paperback)

Disclaimer

This is a work of fiction. Names, characters, places, and incidents are either the product of the author's imagination or used fictitiously. Any resemblance to actual persons, living or dead, or actual events is purely coincidental.

The author and publisher expressly disclaim any responsibility or liability for any loss, injury, adverse effects, or damages—direct or indirect—that may result from the use or application of any information, suggestions, or ideas presented in this book. Readers assume full responsibility for how they choose to use the information contained herein.

All product names, trademarks, and registered trademarks mentioned in this book are the property of their respective owners and are used for identification and educational purposes only. No endorsement is implied. Any products mentioned are used solely as illustrative examples as nominative fair use.

Acknowledgements

Thank you to my sister who listens to my many stories with interest.

No time machines were harmed—though several possibilities were examined.

This book exists because of curiosity, good conversations, judgment, purpose, and the quiet patience of people who allowed imagination to evolve.

Dedication

This book is dedicated to everyone who has ever tried to understand storytelling—and how—you choose to tell it.

To everyone who has ever wondered
what it means to live alongside possible futures.

For those who still pause
before accepting an answer.

Author's Intent

This story explores a simple question with complex consequences:

What if time is not meant to be solved but continuously understood?

We often search for optimal outcomes, stable answers, and permanent solutions.
But systems—biological, technological, and human—rarely thrive under permanence alone.

Stability was never about control.
It was about participation.

Reality was not rewritten by observation.
It was completed by it.

Contents

Preface: The Conversation Has Already Begun

There are moments that seem to repeat. Sometimes again, and again.

Not in exact detail, and not in a way that can be proven—but in the quiet recognition that something has occurred before, or almost before, or in a way that should have already resolved.

We tend to dismiss these impressions.

We call them coincidence, habit, or memory misaligned with the present. We trust continuity. We assume that time moves forward, that events conclude, that decisions—once made—remain made.

But what if that is not always the case?

What if repetition is not error, but evidence?

The London Recurrence explores a condition in which events do not fully resolve. Not because they cannot, but because something within them remains incomplete. The result is not a loop in the conventional sense, but a structure that continues to reattempt alignment—subtly, persistently, and without final confirmation.

In such a system, familiarity becomes unreliable.

Recognition precedes understanding.

And what appears to repeat may, in fact, be an accumulation of attempts that have not yet found agreement.

This is not a story about returning to the same moment.

It is a story about why that moment does not end.

How to Read This Book

This novel is structured as a sequence of moments.

Each chapter is not just a scene—
it is a decision boundary.

You can experience it in different ways:

- **Visually** → Imagine each chapter as a scene unfolding in real time
- **Linearly** → Follow the story from beginning to end
- **Conceptually** → Focus on the system beneath the narrative

The structure is intentional.

Time, decisions, and outcomes matter.

Short chapters reflect transition.
Not brevity.

Pauses matter.
Repetition matters.
Perspective matters.

If you find yourself slowing down—
pausing—
or rereading a line—

the book is working as intended.

Because the most important moments in this story
are not the ones that move forward.

They are the ones that make you stop.

Dramatis Personae

Søren Vahl (record fragmented)
Role: The one who returns; an observer caught within repeating structures that do not complete.
Observed Function: Re-enters similar sequences with slight variation; retains partial awareness across iterations without full continuity.
Visual Identity: A solitary male traveler with a controlled but unsettled presence, wearing a long dark coat. His movements are natural but carry hesitation, as if recognizing patterns before they occur. He can alter how the device interacts with the system.

Elias Vane (pre-convergent state)
Role: The one who precedes alignment; a presence not yet fixed within a single outcome.

Observed Function: Appears intermittently across recurring sequences; introduces deviation within otherwise repeating structures.
Relationship to Søren: Recognition occurs without shared history; interaction disrupts recurrence stability.
Visual Identity: A composed figure whose presence is consistent, though his timing and position do not always align with the surrounding sequence.

The Repeating Woman (designation unconfirmed)
Role: The one who completes the pattern.
Observed Function: Reappears across iterations with minimal variation; maintains continuity within localized loops.
State: Stable within recurrence; not observed to deviate.
Visual Identity: A familiar figure encountered repeatedly in similar positions and actions, unchanged across cycles.

The System (recursive construct)
Role: A structure that attempts resolution through repetition.
Observed Function: Replays sequences with minor variation in an effort to achieve stable continuity; does not finalize outcomes.
State: Active but unresolved; recurrence increases under failed convergence.

Residual Observers (aligned participants)
Role: Sustain environmental continuity through consistent behavior.
Observed Function: Repeat actions across sequences without awareness of prior iterations.
Condition: Fully aligned with each loop; unaffected by recurrence awareness.

The City (London) (recurring environment)
Role: A stable frame for repeated sequences.
Observed Function: Maintains visual and structural consistency across iterations while underlying events subtly vary.
Condition: Externally unchanged; internally unstable.

Trafalgar Square (primary node)
Role: A central recurrence point.
Observed Function: Serves as a repeated site of arrival and observation;

sequence variations frequently originate or reset here.
Properties: Spatially consistent; temporally unstable.

Nelson's Column (fixed reference)
Role: A vertical constant within recurrence.
Observed Function: Provides a stable point of orientation across iterations; unaffected by sequence variation.
Interpretation: Serves as a structural anchor independent of outcome.

The Hotel Room (localized loop)
Role: A contained environment for repeated interaction.
Observed Function: Exhibits subtle changes across iterations (object placement, temporal sequence); suggests incomplete reset between cycles.
Condition: Physically stable; temporally inconsistent.

The Market (variation field)
Role: A dynamic environment where recurrence is less exact.
Observed Function: Displays minor deviations across iterations; serves as a site where variation becomes observable.
Condition: Semi-stable; influenced by observer interaction.

The Briefcase (persistent object)
Role: A constant carried across iterations.
Observed Function: Maintains continuity between sequences; unaffected by local variation.
Condition: Intact; contents not fully observed.

The Notebook (partial record)
Role: A fragmented memory aid.
Observed Function: Contains observations that do not fully correspond to the current iteration; suggests prior awareness.
Limitation: Incomplete; entries may originate from previous cycles.

The Recurrence (structural condition)
Role: A failure to resolve.
Observed Function: Repeats sequences with incremental variation; does not converge to a final state.
Interpretation: Not a loop by design, but by necessity.

Prologue: Not Finishing

THE LONDON RECURRENCE

The Refusal of Time

London had already decided what it was.

Not in any final sense, but in the way a place settles into itself through repetition. Streets held their lines. Buildings maintained their edges. The city moved with the quiet certainty of something that had existed long enough to stop questioning its own structure.

At that hour before full morning, Trafalgar Square lay open and nearly empty beneath a pale sky that had not fully committed to dawn. The stone still carried the memory of rain. Light rested softly across the square without direction, suspended between night and morning as though the city itself had paused before continuing.

Søren Vahl crossed the square without urgency. The London streets felt quietly familiar. He had been here before. Not in any way that could be measured reliably, and not always under the same conditions. Sometimes the briefcase had been in his left hand. Sometimes in his right. Once, he was almost certain he had arrived without it at all. The details resisted consistency. Yet the recognition remained—not as memory, but as alignment. The spacing of the ground. The distance to the steps. The angle of the column against the dim London sky.

He adjusted his path slightly as he walked. The movement felt familiar in a way that unsettled him. Not because he remembered making it, but because somewhere, in some variation of the morning, he already had. Nothing reacted.

The city remained perfectly composed around him. The column stood unchanged. The wet pavement reflected only the pale suggestion of dawn. A bus moved in the distance beyond the square, its sound softened by the hour. And yet something failed to complete.

Søren slowed almost imperceptibly. He looked ahead, then briefly behind him, though he could not have said exactly what he expected to find. Trafalgar Square remained as it was… quiet, symmetrical, stable.

But the moment itself did not close. A fraction of it remained open behind him, subtle enough to escape observation yet impossible to ignore once felt. Not visible. Not measurable. Simply present, as though the city had attempted to finish something and stopped just short of resolution.

He exhaled slowly. This was not repetition. Not exactly. London was not replaying itself in loops or fragments. It was doing something far more precise... and far more unsettling. It was attempting alignment. And somewhere within that attempt, something continued to arrive incorrectly.

Søren continued forward. The light did not shift. The column did not move. The square held its structure perfectly. Only the moment behind him remained unresolved.

He paused, set his briefcase down, and carefully observed the buildings, lights, and street. A flash of memory returned from a time when he had not carried a briefcase. That had been dangerous, uncontrolled, and long ago.

The street looked familiar, but something was wrong. Why had he returned here again?

Imagine.

You arrive without warning—no machine, no explanation—
standing alone, a briefcase in your hand.

The city is silent.

No crowds.
No footsteps but your own.
No one noticed your arrival.

And yet… something is wrong.
You are not meant to be here.
And still…you are not alone.

A memory begins to surface—slowly, uncertainly.

You are a time traveler.
But the memory fractures almost immediately.
Because you feel something else.

You have been here before.

Not in the way memory works.
Not in the way places are learned.

In the way a moment repeats
without permission.

Now… consider the possibilities.
Consider which events chose them.
And then, perhaps, choose another.

Chapter 1: The Return to Trafalgar Square

London was still withholding itself.

Before sunrise, Trafalgar Square lay in a hush of cold stone and suspended light, the broad surface of the plaza darkened by recent rain. Water clung in shallow films across the paving, catching the weak blue-gray of morning and returning it in broken reflections. The city had not yet decided to become filled with activity and noise. Even the buses beyond the square seemed distant, as if passing through another version of the hour.

At the center of it all, Nelson's Column rose into the dim air with the stillness of something that had already outlasted explanation.

Søren Vahl walked toward it alone.

His coat moved only slightly as he crossed the wet stone, long and dark and difficult to place in any single decade. In one hand he carried a weathered briefcase whose leather had lost the vanity of polish years ago and kept only use. His face revealed very little to the morning. Calm, intelligent, restrained. A man who had learned that surprise was often only delayed recognition.

He had been here before. Many times. And each time, something had been slightly different. He did not yet know whether that sentence came from memory or from deduction. By now, the distinction had become unreliable.

The square opened before him in hard geometry—steps, fountains, plinths, the dark forms of the lions still holding their positions in the half-light. Beyond the square, the city waited in a patient arrangement of facades, lamp glow, and unlit windows. London at this hour did not feel like a city waking. It felt like a system pausing.

He slowed near the base of the open expanse and looked up.

Nelson's Column did not invite interpretation. It did not charm. It did not glow. It stood in the center of the square with an authority so complete it seemed to belong not only to London but to recurrence itself. Vertical. Fixed. Measured. A line driven upward through the soft instability of human history.

Søren remained still for a long moment. Nothing happened. That, too, was familiar. He lowered his gaze and studied the pavement instead. Rainwater had gathered in the seams between stones and along slight variations in the grade. Reflections of distant lamps trembled there, thin and imperfect. In one narrow pool, the column appeared broken into pieces by ripples from no visible source.

He kept walking.

His shoes made almost no sound against the wet ground. The briefcase at his side seemed lighter than it should have been, which worried him more than weight ever did. Some places made the device inside it feel heavy, as though time itself thickened around its casing. Other places did the opposite. They reduced apparent mass. They thinned consequence. They encouraged movement.

Those were the dangerous places.

He passed one of the fountain basins and caught the scent of rain on stone, cold metal, and the faint residual smoke of a city that had not entirely finished being night. A gull cried somewhere high above the square. A traffic signal changed color in the distance with no one to obey it. The world remained externally ordinary, and he had learned long ago that ordinary was often the first layer of selection.

His grip tightened fractionally on the briefcase.

The last confirmed sequence had ended in Edinburgh.

Or perhaps in Prague.

That uncertainty annoyed him more than it frightened him. He disliked blurred transitions, missing time intervals, and the kind of memory that arrived already edited. He had written notes to himself for years—some in notebooks, some on receipts, some scratched into materials never meant to hold language. He trusted those notes only slightly more than he trusted his own recollections.

What he knew with certainty was this:
London had begun to recur.
Not in stories. Not metaphorically. Not as emotional repetition or trauma returning in new form. Structurally. Spatially. Measurably. He had seen streets maintain the same pedestrian sequence across different days. Heard the same unfinished sentence in two voices hours apart. Watched a bus cross the edge of his vision twice without reversing direction. Small things at first. Then larger ones. Enough to trace. Enough to return for. An older memory surfaced briefly—a glimpse before the square was constructed.

He stopped again near the centerline of the square. At this distance, Nelson's Column no longer read as monument. It read as instrument.

That thought did not surprise him.

Too many cities hid their true function inside symbols people had forgotten how to read. Churches that were also acoustic markers. Bridges that held not just weight but sequence stress. Towers that behaved like tuned interruptions in continuity. Human beings were very good at inheriting systems they no longer believed themselves capable of constructing.

A breeze moved across the square.

The surface of the nearest puddle shifted.

For the briefest fraction of a second, the reflection inside it showed the column in full daylight while the world around him remained in blue dawn.

Søren did not move. The image vanished at once, resolving into the pale morning again. But the error had occurred. Small. Precise. Enough.

He looked over his shoulder.

No one nearby. A maintenance worker far off near one corner of the square. Headlights turning somewhere beyond the National Gallery. A pair of early pedestrians descending steps without urgency. None of them appeared to notice anything unusual. That was consistent with prior observations. Recurrence rarely announced itself to those not already participating in its pressure.

He turned back toward the column.

The latch on the briefcase clicked once.

Not open.

Awake.

Søren exhaled through his nose, slowly.

He did not kneel. He did not reach for the clasps. He did not make the mistake of interpreting activation as instruction. That error belonged to younger versions of himself, or perhaps to other travelers entirely. By now he understood that the device did not merely respond to anomalies. It amplified relationships between them. Opened too early, it tended to convert observation into commitment.

He preferred not to commit while the square was still making up its mind.

He walked a little farther, angling so the column remained centered in his view while the eastern edge of the city began to brighten. Light gathered slowly behind the architecture, outlining stone and cornice, tracing damp surfaces with a colder silver than Paris had ever offered him. London did not unfold. It clarified.

He paused once more.

This time the delay came in sound.

Somewhere behind him, a single footstep landed.

Then landed again.

Not an echo. Not acoustics. The second impact carried a slightly different weight, as if made by the same person under altered conditions.

He turned.

The square behind him was almost empty.

The two distant pedestrians continued downward, each step ordinary. The maintenance worker had bent to adjust something near a barrier. No one near enough. No one plausible.

Yet the double step had been real.

Søren looked back toward the center of the square and found himself thinking, not for the first time, that recurrence did not begin with repetition. It began with confidence. The environment learned to repeat only after it became certain it had been recognized.

Nothing here felt new.

Not even the morning.

He took out a small notebook from the inner pocket of his coat, opened it to a blank page, and wrote in a hand so controlled it almost looked mechanical:

Trafalgar Square. Pre-sunrise. Wet stone. Column active as reference axis. Sound doubled before visible repetition. Device responsive but not yet opened.

He closed the notebook and put it away.

When he lifted his head again, the light had advanced by only a narrow degree. The city remained in suspension. Nelson's Column stood exactly where it should. The square held. Space and time were holding.

But somewhere inside that holding, Søren felt it: not instability, not fracture, but arrangement. The subtle pressure of a sequence preparing to present itself once more, to see whether he would follow it as he had before. Certain events were important, some were less.

He adjusted the briefcase in his hand and continued walking across the wet stone toward the column, not because he trusted the path ahead, but because mistrust, if precise enough, could also become a form of navigation. He closed his eyes for a moment and took a deep breath.

And as London slowly gathered itself around him, he had the unmistakable sensation that the city was not waiting to be discovered.

It was waiting to see whether he would remember it first.

Chapter 2: The Repeated Morning

The change began in light.

Not in brightness. Not in weather. In arrangement.

Søren noticed it first in shadow, which was where he usually noticed everything that mattered. The base of Nelson's Column cast a narrow angled form across the damp stone, softened at the edges by the hour and by thin vapor lifting from the square. He watched that shadow lengthen by what should have been a natural degree as dawn gathered behind the city.

Then, without the sun visibly advancing, a second shadow formed beside it.

Slightly offset.

Not enough to make a spectacle of itself. Enough to make the first impossible.

He stopped. He could feel cold rain slipping beneath his coat collar.

The plaza ahead remained empty in all the ways an ordinary observer would count emptiness. Open ground. Wet surfaces. Monument. Fountains not yet animated by crowd or chatter. Yet within that emptiness, alignment had begun to duplicate itself. One line of morning overlaid another. One version of illumination arrived before the first had completed its claim.

Søren did not reach for the briefcase. He had learned, at cost, that the first recurrence often revealed more when left uninterpreted.

A gull crossed the pale air above the square. For a moment its shadow split cleanly on the stone below, becoming two wingspans moving at slightly different speeds. Then it resolved back into one.

He lowered his gaze to the pavement.

Rainwater had settled into shallow planes over the stone, turning the square into a broken sheet of reflection. In one pool, the eastern light appeared gray-blue, correct for the hour. In the next, it had already warmed by several minutes. In a third, the surface showed no sky at all—only the column and the dark lion at its base beneath a tone of light that belonged to later morning.

He crouched. He thought for a moment, and rubbed the beard stubble of his chin.

The cold dampness of the stone rose through the fabric at his knee. He studied the three reflections without touching the water. The error was elegant. No tearing. No visible distortion. The world was not cracking. It was layering.

A bus moved along the far edge of the square. He heard it once.

Then, after a pause too exact to be random, heard the same passing weight a second time.

This time he looked up immediately. Only one bus.

Its red body slipped behind the architecture, disappeared, and was gone.

Søren straightened slowly.

Recurrence in London did not behave like bleed-through elsewhere. It lacked spectacle. No ghosted duplicates crossing open plazas. No theatrical flicker in the air. No easy proof. The city repeated itself with the restraint of habit. Events did not fracture. They reasserted themselves.

That made them harder to deny.

A man in a dark coat entered the square from the northwest corner, walking briskly with the posture of someone late for a train or a meeting or an argument. Søren watched him descend three steps, turn slightly, and look at his watch.

Then the same man appeared again at the edge of the square and repeated the descent.

Not another man. The same one. Same coat. Same pace. Same quick checking motion at the wrist.

Søren's expression did not change, but something inside him narrowed to focus.

The first version continued downward.

The second remained two beats behind.

Neither acknowledged the other.

At the third step, the later version failed to complete.

He did not vanish. He thinned. Not visually, not all at once, but structurally. One shoulder lost confidence, then the outline of the coat, then the mass of him returned to the ordinary figure already crossing the square below.

A clean overwrite.

Søren took one step backward, more from thought than fear.

The briefcase clicked again.

He ignored it.

Near one of the fountains, a maintenance cart rolled into view. Its tires hissed faintly over damp stone. The worker guiding it wore a fluorescent jacket too modern for Søren's liking, but the cart itself moved with the same unremarkable pace one would expect at this hour.

Then the cart repeated the same three meters of motion.

Not from the beginning. Just the segment. Forward, slight wobble, correction, hiss of tire, again.

The worker frowned, glanced at a wheel, and kept going.

So.

Not everyone was entirely blind to it. Most simply lacked the framework to name what they experienced.

Søren walked toward the base of the column, angling so that the monument, the fountains, and the eastern approach remained within his view at once. He preferred multiple reference points when a city began to assert duplicate sequence. One object could mislead. Three produced pattern.

The stone lions sat in their familiar stillness, dark with moisture, their surfaces catching the first reluctant hints of warmer light. One of them reflected in a long wet plane across the pavement. Søren paused beside that reflection and watched the earthen-black shape steady itself inside the water.

In the reflected image, a figure crossed behind him.

He did not turn at once. He watched the puddle instead. A man. Long dark coat. Briefcase. Controlled stride.

His own reflection remained where it should have been, facing the opposite direction.

The crossing figure did not glance toward him. It moved through the mirrored world with an assurance that implied prior use, passed behind the reflected lion, and continued across the surface of the water until the thin film trembled under a real-world breeze and erased him completely.

Only then did Søren turn.

Nothing behind him except wet stone, fountain edge, early traffic beyond the square, and the growing light.

Not the first time, then.

The thought arrived with no drama. Merely confirmation.

He slipped a hand into his coat pocket and withdrew the notebook again. On the page beneath his first observation, he wrote:

Morning not merely delayed. Re-presented. Human sequence duplicate observed. Environmental segment duplicate observed. Reflection produced independent crossing figure. Same coat. Same case. Likely me.

He paused, then added:

London repeats by assertion, not by fracture.

That felt right.

He closed the notebook and stood very still, listening.

The city was beginning to wake in earnest now. Engines farther out. A low mechanical pulse from somewhere beneath the square. Doors opening. A voice in the distance. Yet woven through those ordinary sounds he could hear the other layer: tiny reinforcements, repeated impacts, slight returns. The sound of a city practicing itself.

The column remained fixed at the center of all of it.

Søren looked up once more toward the statue high above.

If Paris had always seemed to him like a place where sequences met in atmosphere—through light, scent, and recognition—London was different. London preserved recurrence inside structure. Stone. Steps. Axes. Institutional memory. It did not ask whether an event wished to happen again. It simply provided the conditions under which repetition could become authoritative.

That made the city more dangerous.

He turned away from the column and began to cross the square toward the eastern side, where the streets narrowed and the day would soon commit itself to motion. He did not hurry. Haste, he had found, often caused the environment to simplify around him, and simplification was one of the system's favorite deceptions.

A movement at the edge of his vision caught his attention.

Near the upper steps, a woman in a long dark coat stood for a moment facing the square. Too far away to identify. Too still to ignore.

Søren stopped. He let out a deliberate slow breath as he watched.

She lifted one hand slightly—not waving, not signaling, merely adjusting the angle of something she carried.

A briefcase.

Then a red double-decker bus crossed between them.

When it passed, the steps were empty.

He said nothing.

The recurrence had widened.

Not enough to tell him what it wanted. Enough to tell him that London had moved beyond environmental duplication into presentation. Figures now. Carriers. Repetitions aware enough to stand where he could see them and then withdraw.

He adjusted his grip on the briefcase and continued toward the street beyond the square.

The sky behind the city had finally begun to pale toward a real morning. The shadows narrowed. The duplicated lines on the pavement dissolved back into one. The ordinary world was winning again, or appearing to.

But Søren knew better. Morning was not occurring. It was being selected.

And somewhere ahead... in a room, or a market, or beside a river, or inside one of the city's hidden architectural lungs... the next recurrence was already arranging itself with the confidence of something that had succeeded before.

He left Trafalgar Square without looking back.

Not because he had seen enough. Because London had.

Chapter 3: The Townhouse Window

The street accepted him without question.

That, more than anything, confirmed he was expected.

Søren Vahl turned off the open geometry of Trafalgar Square into a narrower London street where the scale shifted immediately... facades closer, windows taller, the sound of the city compressed into a more deliberate rhythm. The early hour persisted, but here it felt less suspended and more contained, as if the morning had already been filed into place.

He walked past a row of townhouses, each nearly identical in proportion, each carrying small variations that suggested ownership without ever breaking the continuity of the street. Black iron railings. Stone steps. Polished brass fixtures dulled by weather and touch. Doors painted in restrained colors that resisted attention.

He slowed.

Third door from the corner.

Dark green.

Brass handle worn along a single arc.

He did not remember choosing it. He did not remember not choosing it.

He approached the steps and stopped at the base, studying the entrance without touching it. The air here held a different density—less open than the square, more intentional. Spaces like this tended to accumulate sequence. Repetition preferred containment.

His hand rose and hovered near the door.

The briefcase at his side shifted weight, almost imperceptibly.

He waited.

No sound from inside. No movement behind the glass. No signal beyond the quiet persistence of the street itself.

He turned the handle.

Unlocked.

Of course.

He entered without hesitation.

The interior received him with the same restraint as the exterior. A narrow hallway extended forward, floored in dark wood that reflected a muted version of the light filtering through the front glass. A coat rack stood to the right. A small table to the left held nothing but a single folded piece of paper.

He did not touch it.

Not yet.

Instead, he closed the door behind him and remained still.

The house made no effort to conceal itself. No creak of surprise, no shift in air pressure, no delayed reaction to his presence. It behaved as though he had just returned from a brief absence rather than arrived for the first time.

That was always the most difficult condition to evaluate.

He stepped forward.

The wood beneath his feet did not echo. It absorbed.

At the end of the hallway, a doorway opened into a larger room. Light gathered there in a soft gradient, drawn from a tall window that overlooked the street. Søren moved toward it slowly, allowing his eyes to adjust not to brightness, but to arrangement.

The room was complete.

Not furnished.

Complete.

A chair positioned at an angle that suggested recent use. A small table with a glass placed precisely off-center, leaving space for a second that had not been filled. A coat draped across the back of the chair... not his, but close enough in color and cut to feel like an echo.

He stopped just inside the room.

This was not staging.

This was continuation.

He moved to the window.

Outside, the street remained quiet. A car passed, its motion singular. A pedestrian walked along the opposite side, head slightly lowered against the lingering cold. Nothing repeated. Nothing fractured. From here, London behaved exactly as it should.

He placed one hand lightly on the window frame.

The wood was warm.

Not from sunlight.

From prior contact.

He withdrew his hand immediately.

The distinction mattered.

Warmth implied presence.

Presence implied sequence.

He turned slowly, scanning the room again... not for objects, but for alignment. The chair. The table. The glass. The coat. Each element held position with a quiet certainty that suggested they had already been used to confirm something.

The folded paper on the hallway table returned to his thoughts.

He stepped back into the corridor and approached it with care.

The paper was unmarked on the outside.

No name. No date. No instruction.

He picked it up.

The weight was wrong.

Too light.

He unfolded it.

Blank.

He did not react.

Instead, he turned it over and held it at a slight angle to the light.

Indentation.

Pressure marks from writing that had been removed or transferred.

He did not attempt to read it.

That would come later, with the right conditions.

For now, it was enough to know that the house had recorded something and then chosen not to show it.

He refolded the paper and placed it back exactly where it had been.

Not because he wished to preserve the scene.

Because he wanted to see whether the scene would preserve itself.

He returned to the room and stood again at the window.

This time, he did not look outside.

He watched the glass.

For a long moment, nothing happened.

Then...

A figure appeared behind him.

Not in the room.

In the reflection.

Søren did not turn.

The figure stood near the chair, partially obscured by the angle of the room and the distortion of the glass. Long coat. Briefcase. Still posture.

His own outline remained where it should have been.

The second figure did not move.

Did not approach.

Did not vanish.

It simply stood within the reflected space, occupying a position the room itself seemed prepared to accept.

Søren exhaled slowly.

"Not yet," he said quietly, though he did not know whether he was speaking to the figure, the room, or himself.

The reflection held.

Then, without transition, it resolved back into a single image.

He turned.

The room was empty.

Of course.

He crossed to the chair and touched the coat draped over it.

Cool.

Untouched.

Or reset.

He withdrew his hand and stepped back.

This house did not belong to him.

It belonged to the sequence.

And the sequence had already passed through it.

He picked up his briefcase and moved toward the door.

As he reached for the handle, he paused.

Behind him, from the room, came the faintest sound...

A glass being set down.

He closed his eyes for a fraction of a second.

Then opened the door and stepped back into the London morning.

Chapter 4: The Mirror Delay

The street had advanced.

Not dramatically.

Just enough.

Light had strengthened along the upper edges of the buildings, tracing window frames and stonework with a clearer definition than before. The air had lost some of its early heaviness. Sound had returned in layers... distant engines, the low rhythm of movement, the beginning of voices.

London was committing.

Søren did not trust it.

He walked without urgency, turning down a side street that narrowed further, drawing him away from the open lines of the square and into a more controlled environment. These were the spaces where sequence revealed its finer adjustments—less spectacle, more precision.

He found the mirror in a small shop window.

Not displayed.

Installed.

A tall pane set into the glass, framed in dark wood, reflecting the street with a clarity that exceeded its surroundings. The shop itself appeared closed, its interior dim, its purpose unclear. The mirror did not advertise. It observed.

Søren stopped in front of it.

His reflection returned immediately.

Centered. Accurate. Unremarkable.

He watched himself for several seconds without moving.

Then he raised his hand.

In the reflection, the hand rose...

Late.

Not visibly.

Not in a way that would draw attention from anyone passing by.

But to him, the delay was absolute.

He lowered his hand.

The reflection completed the motion after he had already finished it.

He repeated the action.

This time, he slowed the movement, extending the interval between intention and execution.

The reflection followed...

But not exactly.

It did not lag in time.

It lagged in decision.

As though it were not copying him, but arriving at the same action through a separate process.

Søren leaned slightly closer to the glass.

His face in the reflection held steady, but something beneath the surface—an alignment, a structure—felt misregistered.

"You're not behind," he said quietly.

The reflection did not answer.

Of course.

But it did not dismiss the statement either.

A woman passed behind him on the sidewalk, her reflection crossing the mirror cleanly, without delay, without duplication. She glanced at the window briefly, then continued on, unaware of any inconsistency.

So.

Selective.

The system was not applying uniformly.

It was focusing.

On him.

He stepped back.

The reflection remained aligned now, as though the error had been corrected or withdrawn.

That, too, was information.

He turned slightly, shifting his angle to catch both the street and the mirror at once.

Movement in the distance.

A man crossing an intersection.

A cyclist passing behind him.

All normal.

He returned his gaze to the glass.

For a moment, nothing.

Then...

His reflection blinked.

He had not.

Søren did not react outwardly.

Internally, the structure of the observation locked into place.

Independent action.

Not delay.

Not duplication.

Autonomy.

The reflection was not failing to keep up.

It was operating on its own sequence. That made it dangerous.

He stepped closer again, reducing the distance until only a thin layer of glass separated him from the other version of himself.

"Which one are you following?" he asked.

Silence.

The reflected Søren held his gaze.

Then, slowly—deliberately—it tilted its head.

Not mirroring.

Choosing.

A precise, controlled deviation from symmetry.

Søren felt a brief, sharp clarity.

This was not a passive system.

It was evaluating.

Testing alignment.

Measuring response.

He did not tilt his head in return.

He did nothing.

The reflection held the angle for a moment longer.

Then corrected.

Returning to perfect symmetry.

The surface of the glass flattened into ordinary reflection once more.

A bus passed behind him, its red body cutting through the frame. The sound of it matched the motion exactly. No duplication. No delay.

The street had stabilized again.

Or pretended to.

Søren stepped away from the window.

He did not look back.

The mirror had given him what he needed.

Not confirmation of recurrence—that had already been established.

Something else.

Something more precise.

London was not only repeating.

It was **comparing**.

And somewhere within that comparison, it had begun to isolate him as a variable worth testing.

He adjusted the position of the briefcase in his hand and continued down the street.

The city moved around him with increasing confidence. Shops preparing to open. Footsteps aligning into patterns of routine. Voices layering into something that would soon become indistinguishable from normal life.

But Søren carried the image with him:

A version of himself that did not wait for him to move.

A version that acted.

Not incorrectly.

Just… independently.

He turned a corner and disappeared into the deeper structure of London, where the streets tightened and the morning lost its softness.

Behind him, in the quiet shop window, the mirror held its position, reflecting a street that no longer contained him.

Or perhaps...

Contained him twice.

Chapter 5: The Market Near Covent Garden

The streets tightened into motion.

By the time Søren reached the edges of Covent Garden, London had committed to the day. Not loudly—London rarely did anything loudly at first—but with enough certainty that the earlier suspension of time gave way to something more structured. Deliveries. Doors opening. The low, constant hum of preparation.

Markets were ideal.

Not because they were chaotic... but because they were patterned.

He entered without slowing.

The space unfolded in layers: stalls arranged in deliberate proximity, produce laid out in colors that suggested abundance but followed predictable geometry, voices rising and falling within narrow ranges of tone and repetition. Citrus stacked in pyramids. Bread arranged in rows. Flowers positioned to draw the eye in controlled bursts of color.

Søren moved through it like a surveyor.

Not observing the objects.

Observing the intervals.

A vendor reached for an orange.

Paused.

Adjusted the position of a crate.

Then reached again.

Three motions.

Then...

The same three motions repeated.

Not from the beginning.

From the middle.

He stopped.

The vendor did not notice.

No one did.

The repetition was embedded inside the action, not layered over it. It did not announce itself. It completed itself.

Søren shifted his position slightly, aligning his view across multiple stalls.

Patterns emerged.

A woman selecting apples moved her hand across the display, hesitated at the third fruit, chose the second.

Moments later, the same hesitation occurred again—same position, same correction.

A man paying for bread placed coins on the table, adjusted one, then adjusted it again in the exact same way.

Not similar.

Exact.

Søren stepped forward.

The crowd moved around him without resistance, parting just enough to allow passage. Not consciously. Structurally. As if the space recognized his path before he did.

He approached a stall where oranges and loaves of bread were arranged with near-perfect symmetry.

The vendor behind it was older, his posture relaxed but precise, his hands moving with the economy of someone who had performed the same actions for decades.

Søren waited.

The vendor looked up.

Their eyes met.

For a moment, nothing passed between them.

Then the vendor smiled slightly.

"Morning," he said.

Søren did not respond.

Not yet.

He stepped closer, placing himself within the narrow zone where transaction would normally begin.

The vendor reached for an orange.

Stopped.

Looked at Søren again.

"You'll take the bread," he said.

Not as a question.

As a correction.

Søren tilted his head slightly.

"I haven't decided," he replied.

The vendor's expression did not change.

"Yes, you have," he said calmly. "You just haven't said it yet."

Søren felt the structure of the moment shift.

Not emotionally.

Mechanically.

"You're answering before I ask," Søren said.

The vendor nodded once, as if confirming something already known.

"You're asking before you speak," he replied.

A clean inversion.

Søren studied him more carefully now.

The man's movements were precise, but not rigid. His breathing was steady. His gaze held without challenge. There was no sign of confusion, no indication that he found anything unusual in the exchange.

"Has this happened before?" Søren asked.

The vendor reached for a loaf of bread.

Placed it on the counter.

Wrapped it in paper with practiced efficiency.

"Everything happens before," he said.

The wrapping motion completed.

Then...

Repeated.

Not from the beginning.

From the fold.

Paper creased again along the same line.

The vendor did not react.

Søren did.

Internally.

The repetition was no longer confined to background behavior. It was occurring within direct interaction.

"You're aware of it," Søren said.

The vendor looked at him.

For the first time, something shifted in his expression.

Not surprise.

Recognition.

"Of what?" the vendor asked.

The question was genuine.

Not evasive.

Søren held his gaze.

"The repetition," he said.

The vendor considered this.

Then shook his head slightly.

"No," he said. "I'm aware of you."

Søren did not move.

The statement landed with more weight than any anomaly he had observed so far.

"Why?" Søren asked.

The vendor's eyes remained steady.

"Because you're not in the right place," he said.

The words were simple.

The implication was not.

Søren glanced down at the counter.

The loaf of bread sat wrapped, exactly as it had been both times.

He had not asked for it.

He had not refused it.

It existed in the space between decision and outcome.

He looked back up.

"What is the right place?" he asked.

The vendor smiled again, but this time there was no warmth in it... only completion.

"You've already been there," he said.

Then he reached for an orange.

Lifted it.

Turned it once in his hand.

And set it down.

No repetition.

The sequence had closed.

Søren stepped back.

The crowd flowed into the space he had occupied, filling it without resistance. A woman moved forward, placed coins on the counter, received a wrapped loaf—one sequence, clean, uninterrupted.

The vendor did not look at Søren again.

He had already moved on.

Søren turned and walked away from the stall, his pace unchanged but his internal alignment shifting rapidly.

The market had done something new.

Not just repeated.

Not just anticipated.

It had responded.

Not to his actions.

To his presence.

He moved through the remaining stalls with increased attention, scanning for further deviations, but the patterns had settled again into background recurrence—small loops, minor duplications, nothing that engaged him directly.

That, too, was a signal.

The system had chosen a point of contact.

Then withdrawn.

Testing complete.

For now.

He exited the market into a narrower street, the noise of the crowd falling behind him in layers. The air felt cooler here, less saturated with human movement, more controlled.

He adjusted his grip on the briefcase.

The device inside remained quiet.

But not inactive.

He could feel it now... not through heat or weight, but through alignment. As if the internal structure had shifted slightly to match something external.

London was no longer presenting anomalies.

It was presenting decisions.

And somewhere ahead, those decisions would require an answer.

Chapter 6: The Answer Before the Question

The street beyond the market narrowed into a corridor of stone and shadow.

Light entered only in angled fragments, slipping between buildings and catching on glass, metal, and polished stone before breaking apart across the ground. What reached the pavement was incomplete... reflected, redirected, reduced to smaller geometries that shifted as Søren moved.

The sound of the market faded behind him.

Not abruptly.

Gradually... voices thinning into distance, the layered noise resolving into something quieter, more contained. Footsteps. A door closing somewhere above. The muted passage of a vehicle on a street he could no longer see.

Søren slowed.

Spaces like this did not diffuse irregularities.

They concentrated them.

If something repeated here, it would not spread outward. It would tighten. Localize. Become harder to ignore.

He adjusted his path slightly, moving closer to the edge of the street. His gaze tracked across surfaces rather than people—windows, railings, the faint sheen of worn stone—watching not for movement, but for timing.

That was where the system revealed itself.

Not in what happened.

But in when.

A man exited a doorway ahead.

He stepped onto the pavement, adjusted his sleeve, and glanced briefly down the street.

The motion was unremarkable.

Clean.

Complete.

Then...

the sleeve adjustment happened again.

Same angle.

Same speed.

Same duration.

Not faster. Not slower.

Identical.

Søren did not stop. He passed within a few feet of the man, his attention fixed not on the repetition itself, but on its placement.

It was not immediate.

There was no overlap.

No echo.

The second motion did not follow the first—it occupied a position within the sequence as if it had always belonged there.

Inserted.

That distinction mattered.

Layered repetition created distortion. It broke continuity.

This did not.

This held.

Søren continued walking.

At the next corner, a small stall had been set up—temporary, unremarkable. A narrow counter, a metal frame, a compact burner beneath a kettle. Coffee. A few pastries arranged without emphasis. The kind of structure that appeared where needed, remained just long enough to serve its function, then disappeared without trace.

He approached without breaking stride.

The vendor looked up before Søren reached the counter.

"Black," he said.

Søren stopped.

He hadn't spoken.

The vendor reached for a cup, poured the coffee in a smooth, practiced motion, and set it down.

"Anything else?"

Søren remained still for a moment, studying him.

"I didn't order," he said.

The vendor blinked once.

Not confusion.

Correction.

A brief recalibration behind the eyes... as if something had shifted just out of alignment.

"Yes," he said. "You did."

Søren watched his hands.

Steady.

Uncertain... but holding position.

"No," Søren replied. "You assumed."

The vendor's fingers hovered above the counter. The pause extended just long enough to be noticed, but not long enough to disrupt the scene.

Then his hand withdrew.

"Sorry," he said. "It's been one of those mornings."

Søren tilted his head slightly.

"Which one?"

The vendor frowned.

"What do you mean?"

"Which morning?" Søren repeated, his voice calm, almost conversational.

The question settled between them.

Not resisted.

Not processed.

Simply...

unsupported.

The vendor's expression shifted, but not toward understanding. Toward uncertainty. The kind that resolves itself by returning to a familiar pattern.

"I don't follow," he said.

Of course he didn't.

Awareness wasn't sustained.

It surfaced.

Localized.

Then collapsed back into sequence.

Søren reached into his pocket and placed coins on the counter. The motion restored the structure of the exchange immediately.

The vendor nodded, relief almost visible.

“Right,” he said. “That’ll do.”

He handed over the coffee.

This time, the interaction completed cleanly.

No anticipation.

No repetition.

No correction.

Søren took the cup.

The heat registered instantly against his hand.

Immediate.

Unmediated.

That mattered more than the exchange itself.

He smelled the coffee and took a sip—then another.

Warm.
Full-bodied.
Appreciated.

It settled slowly, not just on the tongue but deeper—something grounding in the way the heat lingered, the way the bitterness held just long enough before softening.

He didn’t rush the next sip.

He let it come to him.

He stepped away from the stall, moving toward the edge of the street where a narrow side passage opened between two buildings. The light there was thinner, more constrained. The air felt cooler—not colder, but less affected by the surrounding movement.

He paused and looked back.

The vendor was already serving someone else.

No hesitation.

No trace.

The sequence had absorbed the anomaly and continued without residue.

Søren lifted the cup slightly and watched the surface of the coffee.

Still.

No distortion.

No delay.

He took another small sip.

The taste was unremarkable. The same as before.

And because of that, it was exact.

Not repeated.

Not corrected.

Singular.

For the first time since entering the market, he experienced a moment that belonged entirely to itself.

That was the confirmation.

Not failure.

Selection.

The system was not collapsing under strain.

It was choosing.

Certain interactions were isolated—held, repeated, advanced, tested within narrow boundaries.

Others were allowed to pass without interference.

Not everything required correction.

Only what approached instability.

That was the first usable insight.

Not how to control the system.

But how to recognize where it would act.

Søren lowered the cup.

From somewhere deeper within the city, a low mechanical sound emerged—subtle, steady, almost beneath hearing. It did not belong to traffic. Not to anything localized.

It was broader than that.

Structural.

Infrastructure operating at a level not intended to be noticed.

He turned toward the narrow passage.

The alignment shifted as he faced it.

Not externally.

Internally.

As if his position relative to the system had changed again—not where he stood, but how he was being processed within it.

The vendor had answered before he spoke.

The market had responded before he acted.

The reflection had moved before he did.

Sequence was no longer following him.

It was moving ahead of him.

That changed the risk. It became something more dangerous.

If events could anticipate position, then delay would not protect him.

Only awareness of threshold would.

Where sequence transitioned from passive to active—

that was where intervention occurred.

That was where decisions were made.

Søren stepped into the passage without hesitation.

Behind him, the street continued—voices rising, footsteps passing, the city resolving into morning as if nothing had shifted.

Ahead, the space narrowed.

Darkened.

Focused.

And as the light thinned and the corridor closed around him, one realization settled... not as theory, but as position:

He was no longer observing the recurrence.

He had entered the point at which it was decided.

Chapter 7: The Device Opened in Restraint

The passage narrowed until the city became a memory of sound behind him.

At first, it was still there... the distant rhythm of movement, the low hum of traffic, voices rising and falling in indistinct patterns. Then it thinned. Not fading completely, but receding into something less immediate, as if the space itself filtered what could follow him.

Light narrowed with it.

What reached the walls came in angled fragments, slipping between structures above and breaking across damp stone and exposed metal fixtures embedded without ornament. The surfaces did not reflect so much as absorb and redistribute—light arriving intact, leaving altered.

The air cooled gradually.

Not enough to discomfort.

Enough to focus.

Søren slowed.

Spaces like this did not exist by accident. They did not support ordinary movement—they refined it. Removed excess. Reduced variability.

This was where alignment could be measured.

This was where the device mattered.

Not because it would immediately resolve anything.

Because it would confirm position.

He stopped midway down the passage and set the briefcase on a narrow ledge of stone that ran along the wall at waist height.

The surface was worn.

Not by time.

By repetition.

Placement. Contact. Pressure applied in consistent patterns. A point of use, not decay.

Others had stood here.

Or something had.

Søren rested his hand lightly on the case.

Waited.

Nothing immediate.

That was correct.

If the device responded too quickly, it meant it was being driven by input rather than condition. That was unstable.

He left it closed.

For now.

Instead, he studied the passage.

It extended forward another ten meters before bending out of view. No doors. No windows. No interruptions. The kind of architecture that did not declare purpose, but enforced it through constraint.

The floor sloped—barely visible, but enough to suggest direction rather than drainage.

Movement here would not disperse.

It would gather.

A faint vibration passed through the stone beneath his hand.

Subtle.

Rhythmic.

Not mechanical.

Not random.

Søren lifted the case.

The latch clicked once.

Not because he opened it.

Because the condition changed.

He set it back down.

"Not yet," he said quietly—not to the device, but to the moment itself.

The vibration continued.

No escalation.

No decay.

Stable input.

That mattered.

He exhaled slowly and released the clasps.

The briefcase opened with controlled resistance. The hinges absorbed the motion without sound, as if preventing the act itself from introducing disruption.

Inside, the device rested in a fitted structure that held it in precise orientation.

Layered metallic geometry surrounded a central core.

The light was cool.

Steady.

Uninviting.

No flicker.

No surge.

Nothing to suggest activation.

Søren did not touch it.

Not immediately.

He observed.

The internal structure had shifted.

Not dramatically.

But enough.

Outer rings slightly misaligned from their previous configuration. The inner lattice adjusted by fractions too small to detect without familiarity.

He was familiar.

Which meant the device had already begun to respond.

Not to activation. To context.

That was the first rule.

The device did not wait to be used.

It evaluated position continuously.

He placed two fingers lightly against the outer frame.

The response was immediate.

Not visual.

Relational.

The vibration in the stone synchronized with the geometry of the device. The two systems—external and internal—aligned into a shared frequency that traveled through his hand and up his arm.

Not sensation.

Information.

He closed his eyes.

The device did not project.

It did not display.

It aligned.

Patterns formed—not in front of him, but within the structure of his perception. Lines intersecting without fixing. Branches extending without committing to divergence. Paths existing as potential, not outcome.

It was not showing him where to go.

It was showing him where change would occur.

That distinction mattered.

Coordinates would imply control.

This was threshold.

He held contact only as long as needed.

Any longer would introduce bias—forcing interpretation into what was meant to remain conditional.

He withdrew his hand.

The resonance faded immediately.

Good.

The device should never persist beyond interaction.

He studied the core again.

The light remained steady—but not uniform. Subtle fluctuations suggested evaluation rather than output.

The device was not giving direction.

It was measuring deviation.

And now...

recording it.

He closed the case.

Deliberately.

The clasps sealed with a soft, contained finality.

The vibration in the stone continued for a moment longer, then resolved into stillness.

The passage returned to silence.

Søren lifted the briefcase.

The weight had changed.

Slightly heavier.

He did not look at it.

He adjusted his grip.

That was expected.

Not mass.

Accumulation.

The device was not storing data.

It was storing constraint.

Boundaries of stability.

What had been tested.

What had held.

What had nearly failed.

That would matter later.

For him.

For anyone who used it after.

He moved forward.

The passage bent to the right, revealing a continuation that descended more noticeably now. The walls drew closer. The air cooled further. The last trace of the city disappeared completely.

This was no longer transitional space.

This was internal.

He paused at the turn.

Looked back.

The entrance was no longer visible.

Not closed.

Receded.

Distance had changed without corresponding movement.

The space behind him had deprioritized his position.

That was new.

Søren did not react.

Reaction implied misalignment.

He turned and continued.

The device had confirmed what he needed:

London was not repeating.

It was selecting. Not passively. Actively.

And more importantly...

it was no longer responding to him.

It was positioning him.

He adjusted his grip on the case and stepped deeper into the passage.

This was no longer observation.

This was placement.

Chapter 8: Dinner Over the Thames

By the time Søren emerged from the lower passage, London had reached evening.

Not gradually.

Completely.

The transition had not occurred in the sky, or in the visible movement of the city. It had happened somewhere within the structure he had just left—beyond sequence, beyond the ordinary accumulation of time. One moment, the world had held morning. The next, it resolved into dusk.

Lights were already active.

Streetlamps glowed in steady intervals along the embankment. Windows carried warm interior illumination. The sky deepened toward blue and gold, the last traces of daylight receding without having visibly passed.

Movement continued.

Traffic flowed across the bridges in the distance. Pedestrians moved along the river walk in loose, unsynchronized patterns. Nothing appeared interrupted.

Everything appeared continuous.

Søren did not question the shift.

He accepted it as confirmation.

Time, here, was not progressing.

It was being assigned.

He stepped out onto the embankment and paused at the railing.

The Thames moved with its usual measured pace, carrying the reflected city in elongated streaks of light that formed, stretched, and broke as the current advanced. Bridges held their structure across the water—unchanged, stable, precise in their geometry.

On the surface, nothing resisted.

Nothing repeated.

But Søren no longer mistook that for neutrality.

Continuity, he had learned, was the most convincing form of selection.

He turned slightly—and saw it.

A small table had been set near the railing.

White cloth.

Two chairs.

One occupied.

Not by a person.

By absence.

It was not emptiness.

It held position.

Defined space.

The second chair was angled slightly away from the table, as though someone had stood from it moments before—close enough to suggest presence, far enough to imply interruption.

Søren approached.

Stopped a short distance from the table.

The arrangement was precise.

A glass half-filled.

A plate untouched.

Utensils aligned with deliberate care.

No displacement.

No disorder.

Nothing disturbed...

except the chair.

He set the briefcase down beside the empty seat.

Did not sit.

Instead, he moved slowly around the table, examining it from multiple angles. Not looking for duplication, not expecting delay—only observing whether the arrangement held under scrutiny.

It did.

Perfectly.

No echo.

No drift.

No correction.

That, more than anything, made it unstable.

He pulled the empty chair slightly closer to the table.

The movement was small.

Intentional.

He sat.

The wood beneath him was warm.

Not from ambient temperature.

From recent use.

That detail mattered more than the placement.

Someone—or something—had occupied this position.

Recently.

He placed his hands lightly on the table.

The cloth did not shift.

The surface beneath was firm, grounded, entirely present.

He looked across.

At the absence.

At the position that remained filled without form.

"You're ahead of me," he said quietly.

The words did not echo.

They did not distort.

They entered the environment and resolved without resistance.

The river continued its motion.

A boat passed beneath one of the bridges in the distance, its wake briefly disturbing the reflections before they reformed into new patterns.

No response.

Søren did not expect one.

He waited.

Time did not pause.

That, too, was information.

Where the system held structure, it did not suspend progression.

He reached for the glass.

Lifted it.

The liquid inside remained stable—no distortion, no duplication, no anticipatory shift.

He took a sip. And then another.

The taste was precise.

Singular.

Unrepeated.

He set the glass down and watched it.

Nothing followed.

Nothing repeated.

The sequence held exactly once.

That confirmed the condition.

This was not recurrence.

This was presentation.

He ate a piece of sliced bread, still warm, moist, appreciated.

He leaned back slightly in the chair, allowing himself—for the first time since entering London—a moment that was not purely analytical.

The system had changed its method.

Before, it had revealed itself through duplication—through repetition that could not fully integrate.

Now, it was constructing.

Selecting specific configurations.

Holding them in place long enough to be engaged.

Then testing response.

He glanced again at the second chair.

Still angled away.

Still suggesting interruption.

He reached out and adjusted it—bringing it into perfect alignment with the table.

Then he waited.

Nothing.

The chair remained where he placed it.

No correction.

No reset.

The structure held.

Søren exhaled slowly.

So.

Intervention was possible.

But only under certain conditions.

He stood, moving around the table again. This time, he placed his hand on the back of the second chair and held it there, applying steady, deliberate contact—not force, but presence.

He waited.

The system did not react immediately.

That was consistent.

Immediate correction would imply instability.

Delayed response implied evaluation.

He released the chair.

Stepped back.

The arrangement held.

For a moment, longer than expected.

Søren turned away from the table, reaching for the briefcase.

As his hand closed around the handle...

he heard it.

A faint shift.

Behind him.

He turned.

The second chair was angled away again.

Exactly as before.

Not approximate.

Not adjusted.

Restored.

The original configuration had reasserted itself—not as correction, but as priority.

The system had allowed the change to exist.

But not to persist.

That distinction was critical.

Temporary deviation.

Permanent structure.

Søren nodded once.

He understood now.

Change was not forbidden.

But it was conditional.

The system did not resist intervention outright.

It measured it.

Allowed it.

Then determined whether it could remain without destabilizing the larger continuity.

Most changes would not qualify.

He lifted the briefcase.

The weight settled naturally in his hand.

No increase.

No signal.

This had not been a threshold event.

It had been a test.

He stepped away from the table.

Did not look back immediately.

When he did, only briefly, nothing had changed.

The table remained.

Prepared.

Complete.

Occupied by absence.

Waiting.

As he continued along the embankment, the river moving steadily beside him, the city holding its assigned evening, Søren recognized the progression with increasing clarity:

The system was no longer asking what he would observe.

It was testing what he would alter...

and how much of that alteration could be allowed to remain.

Chapter 9: Westminster Bridge Repetition

The embankment carried him forward until the river narrowed into structure.

Ahead, Westminster Bridge stretched across the Thames in a clean, deliberate span. Its lamps were already lit, each one casting a contained halo of warm light that repeated at fixed intervals along the length of the crossing. Beyond it, the Palace of Westminster held the far edge of the city—dark, massive, stable in a way that suggested permanence, whether or not that permanence was real. Big Ben and the iconic views appeared stable.

Søren slowed as he approached the first arch.

Bridges mattered. Not symbolically. Structurally.

They forced continuity. They required agreement between two separate conditions—two sides of a sequence that might otherwise diverge. Movement across them could not fragment without consequence.

That made them ideal for testing.

He stepped onto the bridge.

The surface was damp, carrying a thin sheen of moisture that reflected the lamps in elongated streaks. Each reflection stretched and broke under the passage of vehicles, reforming just long enough to maintain coherence before dissolving again.

The rhythm established itself immediately.

Light. Distance. Shadow. Repetition. A pattern designed to be trusted.

Søren walked along the left side, keeping the railing within reach but not touching it. The metal bars formed a regular vertical sequence—equidistant, stable, predictable.

The first anomaly appeared at the third lamp.

He did not see it directly. He felt it in the timing.

As he passed beneath the light, the halo extended slightly beyond its boundary—overlapping the next interval before retracting into its proper position.

Subtle.

Contained.

If he had not been measuring, he would have missed it.

He stopped.
Turned.
Looked back.

The lamps held steady.

Perfect spacing. Perfect containment. Nothing out of place.

He faced forward again and resumed walking.

At the fifth lamp, the duplication occurred again. More clearly this time.

The light from one fixture occupied two positions within the same interval—not brighter, not distorted—just present twice, briefly, before resolving into singular form.

Søren did not break stride.

He counted.

Sixth—normal.
Seventh—normal.
Eighth...

The railing beside him shifted.

Not physically.

Relationally.

The vertical bars aligned twice, creating a precise double position—two sets occupying the same structure without blurring into one another.

He stopped again. Placed his hand on the metal.

Cold. Solid. Single.

He looked down at the river.

The reflection of the bridge extended across the water in broken lines of gold and black. The current carried them forward, fragmenting and reforming with natural motion.

Then...

one segment repeated.

Not across the surface.

Within it.

A line of reflected light appeared twice in the same current, moving at slightly different speeds, neither displacing the other.

Not reflection.

Repetition.

Søren straightened.

The pattern was now clear. Not random. Not environmental. Segment-based.

The bridge was not repeating as a whole.

It was repeating in parts. Inserted sequences. Controlled intervals.

That meant the system was no longer testing surface-level continuity.

It was testing structural tolerance.

He resumed walking.

Ahead, near the midpoint of the bridge, a figure stood.

Male. Still. Positioned slightly left of center, facing the far end.

Søren did not slow. He had expected something. Not necessarily this.

But something.

The figure did not move. Did not turn.

Did not acknowledge his approach.

As Søren closed the distance, the duplication intensified.

The lamps near the figure began to repeat more frequently—halos overlapping, separating, then collapsing back into singular alignment. The railing formed brief double structures at irregular intervals.

And the sound of his footsteps—

shifted.

Not behind him. Beside him.

A second rhythm, perfectly matched but offset just enough to exist independently.

Søren stopped five meters from the figure.

The duplication ceased.

Immediately.

The bridge returned to singular alignment.

The lamps stabilized. The railing resolved. The sound collapsed into one.

Silence held, broken only by the distant movement of the city.

The figure remained facing away.

Søren studied him. Posture. Height. Stillness. Familiar.

"You've been placed here," Søren said.

The man did not turn.

"Yes," he replied.

The voice was calm. Measured. Known.

Søren's expression did not change.

"By the system," he said.

A slight pause.

Then...

"No," the man said. "By you."

That shifted the frame. Not control. Not placement. Consequence.

Søren stepped forward once.

"Not yet," he said.

The man tilted his head slightly. Not enough to reveal his face. Enough to suggest recognition.

"You always say that," he replied.

"Always."

The word held longer than it should have. Not repeated. Persistent. Søren remained still. The bridge held its alignment.

"Which sequence are you in?" Søren asked.

"The one that holds," the man said.

Søren narrowed his gaze slightly.

"Holds what?" he asked.

"Constraint," the man replied. "Not the moment. The condition that allows it."

Søren studied him.

"So you're not the event," he said. "You're the boundary."

A faint shift in the man's posture.

"Close."

"You're not duplicated," Søren said.

"No."

"Then what I saw before—on the bridge—wasn't you."

"No," the man replied. "That was echo."

Søren paused.

"Define it."

The man did not hesitate.

"Duplication occupies space twice," he said. "Echo occupies time twice."

Søren's expression sharpened.

"And this?" he asked.

"This is alignment without repetition," the man said. "A state that doesn't need to resolve to remain stable."

The man exhaled softly.

"You're measuring access," Søren said.

"I'm measuring consequence," the man replied.

Søren tilted his head slightly.

"You think the opening causes the instability."

"It doesn't cause it," the man said. "It reveals where the system cannot decide."

"You don't trust the opening."

"I trust structure," Søren said.

"You trust control," the man replied.

Søren did not respond.

The man continued:

"The system doesn't break because it lacks precision," he said. "It breaks because it can't choose what to release."

Søren's grip on the briefcase tightened slightly.

"And you think release is the solution."

"I think it's the only thing that prevents accumulation from becoming permanence."

"You're ahead of me," he said.

"No," the man replied. "You're narrowing faster than I did."

Søren's eyes flicked briefly toward the lamps.

"Narrowing what?"

"Possibility," the man said.

A pause.

Then:

"You think alignment means correctness," he continued. "It doesn't."

"What does it mean?"

"That the system has chosen to hold something," the man said. "Not that it should."

"Did you open it?"

Søren felt the briefcase at his side.

Heavier. Not physically. Relationally.

"Yes," he said.

A pause.

"Early?" the man asked.

Søren considered.

Then:

"No."

The man nodded once.

"Good."

The duplication returned.

Not around them.

Between them.

The space separating the two men doubled—not visually, but structurally. The distance existed in two states simultaneously—shorter and longer, accessible and unreachable.

Søren stepped forward. The distance did not change. He stopped.

So.

Movement alone did not resolve position. That was the second usable insight.

The man spoke again.

"It doesn't end here."

"It doesn't end anywhere," Søren said.

The man almost nodded.

"It transitions," he replied. "But not always forward."

Søren stilled.

"Not forward?"

The man finally shifted slightly.

"Alignment can diverge without breaking," he said. "You haven't seen that yet."

Søren held his gaze.

"But you have."

A pause.

"Not here."

Søren's grip tightened on the briefcase.

"Where?" he asked.

A pause.

Then:

"Inside."

The word did not point.

It directed. Not location. Structure.

Søren's grip tightened again on the briefcase.

The man said nothing more.

The bridge remained stable.

The system had paused again—not in time, but in evaluation.

Søren stepped back.

The distance returned to five meters.

Immediately. The duplication reinserted itself.

He nodded once. Understood.

"You're not staying," Søren said.

"No," the man replied.

"Then you're not real."

"That depends on your definition," the man said.

Søren waited.

"Reality is continuity you can't step outside of," the man continued.

"And you?"

"I can step outside of alignment," he said. "Not outside of consequence."

Søren considered that.

"That makes you unstable."

"No," the man replied. "It makes me consistent across states."

Søren's gaze held.

"Consistency without permanence," he said.

The man inclined his head slightly.

"That's what you're about to change."

Søren paused for a fraction longer than necessary.

"One more thing," he said.

The man did not turn.

"When it stops holding—what replaces it?"

A longer silence this time.

Then:

"It doesn't stop," the man said. "It redefines what holding means."

Søren absorbed that.

"And if it can't?"

The man's voice lowered, just slightly.

"Then it stops choosing."

Søren turned. He did not wait.

As he walked toward the far end of the bridge, the duplication diminished—segment by segment—until the structure returned to singular continuity.

He did not look back. He didn't need to. The encounter had provided what mattered. Not answers. Constraints.

The system could:
- place entities
- align them across sequences
- maintain consistency without permanence

And more importantly...

it could test him through them.

Ahead—

inside—

that structure would no longer be implied.

It would be visible.

Chapter 10: The Figure at the Far End

The far side of the bridge received him without resistance.

Traffic passed at a steady pace, headlights tracing brief lines across the damp surface before dissolving into the ambient light of the street. Pedestrians moved along the pavement in loose, uncoordinated patterns—some alone, some in pairs, each following their own timing without visible interference.

Nothing disrupted. Nothing repeated.

The city continued its evening progression as if the bridge behind him had been entirely uneventful.

And yet...

the alignment remained.

Søren felt it not as an external force, but as a subtle recalibration in how the environment responded to him. The intervals between objects. The timing of movement. The way light held just slightly longer before releasing.

The system had not disengaged.

It had repositioned.

He stepped fully onto the pavement beyond the bridge.

The architecture shifted immediately.

The openness of the embankment gave way to vertical constraint. Buildings rose closer together. Windows stacked in narrow columns. Streets tightened, reducing lateral movement and guiding everything forward.

The river disappeared behind him. The city became contained again.

He paused at the corner. Looked ahead.

Another figure stood at the far end of the street.

Not the same as before.

The posture was different—less stable, less deliberate. The build narrower. The stance not as anchored.

Still male. Still. Still waiting.

Søren did not approach immediately.

He watched. The figure did not move. Did not shift weight.

Did not acknowledge the people passing nearby.

Pedestrians adjusted around him—but without awareness. They neither reacted nor avoided him directly. Their paths bent just enough to accommodate his presence, then resumed.

Not avoidance.

Accommodation.

As if the system recognized the figure, even if the individuals within it did not.

Søren stepped forward.

The distance closed normally.

No duplication. No delay. Ten meters. Eight. Five.

The environment held steady.

At three meters, Søren stopped.

"Are you placed?" he asked.

The figure did not respond.

Søren studied him more closely.

The face was visible now.

But not fixed.

Features existed—eyes, mouth, structure—but they did not resolve into identity. Each detail was present, yet none committed fully. A face assembled without conclusion.

"You're not fixed," Søren said.

The figure's head turned slightly.

Finally.

The motion was not delayed.

But it was not entirely continuous either—as if the decision to turn had been evaluated before being executed.

The man's eyes met Søren's.

"You're closer," the man said.

The voice was different from the one on the bridge.

Less stable.

Less certain.

It held—but only just.

Søren did not react.

"To what?" he asked.

The man hesitated.

Not searching for words.

Searching for structure.

"For the point," he said.

"What point?"

The man's expression shifted. For a moment, the features aligned—becoming sharper, more coherent—before softening again.

"The one you change," he said.

Søren felt the alignment tighten.

Not around him.

Within him.

"Where is it?" he asked.

The man's gaze moved past Søren—not toward anything visible, but toward something beyond the immediate structure of the street.

"Below," he said.

Søren held his gaze.

"Below is not location," he said. "It's condition."

The man's features sharpened slightly.

"Yes."

"Then say it correctly," Søren said.

The man struggled—not with meaning, but with form.

"It's where the system stops allowing surface alignment," he said. "Where it has to decide what holds."

Søren stepped closer.

"That implies failure."

The man shook his head.

"No. It implies consequence."

Søren's expression remained steady.

"What's the difference?"

The man answered more quickly this time.

"Failure breaks structure," he said. "Consequence defines it."

A pause.

Søren studied him.

"You're not stable enough to hold that distinction."

"No," the man said. "I'm only here to resolve it."

"Resolve what?"

The man's voice lowered slightly.

"The difference between what repeats and what returns."

Søren's eyes narrowed.

"That's not the same thing."

"No," the man said. "And the system treats them differently."

"Explain."

The man hesitated again.

Then:

"Repetition is unchosen," he said. "Return is selected."

Søren absorbed that.

"Then duplication is failure."

"Yes."

"And echo?"

"Echo is memory that hasn't been released."

Søren's posture shifted slightly.

"And resolution?"

The man's expression almost stabilized.

"Resolution is when the system decides it no longer needs to remember."

A longer pause.

Søren spoke again.

“You’re not the first,” he said.

The man’s gaze flickered—not away, but inward.

“No.”

“How many?”

The man’s face destabilized slightly.

“Not counted,” he said.

“Then how do you know you’re not alone?”

The answer came immediately.

“Because I’m incomplete.”

Søren held that.

“And the others?”

The man’s voice thinned slightly.

“Some hold.”

“Some?”

A pause.

“Some don’t resolve.”

That mattered.

Søren pressed further.

“And when they don’t?”

The man’s form flickered—not visually, structurally.

“They accumulate.”

Søren exhaled slowly.

“And when accumulation exceeds tolerance?”

The man looked directly at him.

"Then something else has to decide."

Søren's grip tightened slightly.

"Something else?"

The man did not answer immediately.

Then...

"Not the system."

A longer silence. Søren understood. Not fully. But enough.

The word carried the same weight as before.

Inside. Below.

Different expressions. Same direction. Consistent.

Søren stepped closer.

Two meters now.

The man's face sharpened again—almost resolving into a recognizable identity. For a brief moment, Søren had the sense that if he focused, if he committed to the recognition, the face would lock into place.

He did not. The features softened. Unresolved.

"You don't hold," Søren said.

The man shook his head.

"No," he replied. "I resolve."

That distinction settled quickly.

The first figure had been stable—persistent across conditions.

This one...

temporary.

A function. Not meant to remain.

"For how long?" Søren asked.

The man did not answer immediately.

When he did, the words were quieter.

"Long enough."

Long enough for what?

Not to exist.

To complete.

That was the difference.

Søren stepped back.

The man's outline shifted—not visually, but structurally. The space he occupied began to lose coherence, as if the environment no longer required his presence.

"You're not the first," the man said.

Søren paused.

That mattered. Sequence implied. Iteration implied. But not repetition.

"Nor are you," Søren replied.

The man's expression almost formed a smile.

Not emotion.

Resolution.

Then...

he was gone.

Not vanished.

Released.

The space closed around where he had stood. Pedestrians continued through it without hesitation. The structure absorbed the absence immediately, restoring continuity without trace.

Søren turned.

The alignment shifted again.

The direction forward no longer extended across the city.

It compressed. Focused. He scanned the street. Not for movement.

For access. Entrances that did not announce themselves. Structures that guided without signaling. He found one.

A narrow descent between two buildings—partially obscured, easily overlooked. The kind of opening that existed only when needed.

Intentional.

Søren moved toward it without hesitation.

Behind him, the city continued its evening progression—lights, movement, sound—all resolving naturally into sequence.

Ahead, the space tightened.

Darkened.

Prepared.

And as he stepped into the descent, one realization settled fully into place:

The system was no longer presenting possibilities.

It was directing him.

Toward the point where change occurred...

and where consequence would no longer be released.

Chapter 11: The Opening Below

The entrance did not resist him.

It narrowed, yes—but not to prevent entry.

To define it.

The buildings pressed inward as Søren approached, their edges tightening the space until the path between them no longer felt like part of the city, but something set apart from it. The transition was not marked by a boundary, or a barrier.

It was marked by removal.

Noise receded first—the distant hum of traffic thinning into something indistinct. Then motion—the layered activity of the city dissolving as if it had only ever been surface-level. And finally, the background continuity itself—the invisible structure that allowed London to function as a whole.

Below, that continuity did not follow.

It was replaced.

Søren stepped into the descent, and the city sealed itself behind him—not by closing, but by no longer including him in its active sequence.

The steps were shallow.

Even.

Worn only where contact had been repeated.

Not age.

Use.

His foot met each surface with quiet consistency. The rhythm required no adjustment. He did not look down. His body recognized the cadence before his attention could.

That recognition unsettled him more than the space.

This had not just been built. It had been used. Repeatedly.

The walls drew inward just enough to remove distraction. No signage. No markings. No variation in texture or structure that might suggest interpretation.

Direction was not offered. It was assumed. And Søren followed it.

The air cooled as he descended—not sharply, but with a controlled reduction that mirrored the earlier passage.

Not identical. But close. Close enough to confirm pattern.

Close enough to suggest that this sequence had been entered before. More than that.

He reached the base of the steps, and the passage opened.

Not into a room.

Into a condition.

The chamber was circular.

Minimal.

Complete.

Its geometry did not present itself as architecture. It did not feel designed. It felt resolved—as if it existed not because it had been constructed, but because no other configuration would remain stable.

At its center stood a single structure.

Not large.

Not imposing.

But exact.

A platform—raised only slightly from the surrounding floor.

Its surface absorbed light rather than reflecting it. The edges did not catch illumination—they dissolved into it, making the boundary perceptible only through absence rather than contrast.

Faint lines traced its perimeter.

They did not repeat.

They did not form a closed pattern.

They extended.

As if the structure continued beyond what could be seen.

Søren stopped at the edge.

This was the point. Not symbolically. Functionally.

He had stood here before. Not as memory. As recognition.

He set the briefcase down beside the platform.

Did not open it. Not yet.

That restraint was no longer instinct.

It was learned.

He knew what happened when timing slipped—when the system engaged before position stabilized.

Instead, he moved.

Slowly.

Deliberately.

He walked around the platform, observing how it responded—not externally, but relationally. The lines embedded in its surface did not shift physically, yet their alignment adjusted as he changed position.

The structure was not fixed. It was responsive. Not to input. To presence.

Each step altered the relationship between him and the platform. Angles that had seemed aligned no longer were. Intersections that had been implied became latent.

The platform was not presenting itself. It was recalculating him.

That was the second rule.

The system did not adapt to the traveler. It evaluated them.

He completed the circle. Returned to his starting position.

Nothing had changed. Everything had changed.

He stepped onto the platform. The effect was immediate.

Not visual. Not auditory. Structural.

The chamber recalibrated—not in size, not in shape, but in reference. The walls did not move, but their relation to him shifted. Distance became conditional. Orientation lost its fixed axis.

The center was no longer a place.

It was him. Søren remained still.

He did not reach for the briefcase.

He did not move to engage.

He waited.

Too early—and the system fractured.

Too late—and it closed.

That had happened before.

He did not intend to repeat it.

He stepped off.

The chamber returned to baseline.

Stable. Contained.

He stepped back on.

Again, the shift.

This time, he held longer.

The lines within the platform began to resolve—not into images, not into instruction, but into relationships. Extensions that implied continuation. Intersections that suggested potential divergence.

Paths. Not chosen. Not yet.

He stepped off again.

Silence returned.

He nodded. Confirmed.

This was not where change occurred.

This was where change was defined.

That distinction mattered more than anything he had encountered so far.

He knelt beside the briefcase.

Rested his hand on it.

The surface felt unchanged.

The implication did not.

The latch responded—not opening, but acknowledging.

Recognition.

"Now," he said.

He opened it.

The device did not activate.

It aligned.

The internal geometry shifted instantly, synchronizing with the structure of the platform. The central core clarified—not brighter, not more intense—but more exact.

Compatibility.

Søren lifted it.

The weight had changed again.

Not physically. Responsibility. The device no longer observed.

It participated.

He stepped back onto the platform.

The chamber responded more strongly this time. The walls receded—not outward, but in relevance. The platform became the only meaningful structure.

Everything else became context.

He adjusted his stance.

Half a step forward.

A slight rotation.

The device in his hand responded immediately. Internal structures shifted. The platform's embedded lines recalibrated.

Closer.

Not complete.

He stopped moving.

That was the third rule.

The system would not guide precision.

It would only respond to it.

He adjusted again.

Smaller this time.

Less intention.

More first alignment.

The geometry held.

And then… something resolved.

Not projected. Not displayed.

A point. Single. Defined.

Suspended between the device and the platform.

It did not emit light.

It did not move.

But it existed.

Søren held his position.

His breathing slowed—not from fear, but from control.

This was the opening. Not a door. Not a passage.

A decision.

Every sequence—every repetition, every alignment, every insertion—had led here.

Not to force action.

To isolate it.

He did not reach for the point. Not yet.

That mistake had been made.

Instead, he studied it. Its position. Its relation to him. To the device. To the platform.

If he moved... even slightly... it would change.

Or disappear. Or become something else.

He adjusted one finger. Barely.

The point trembled. Not visually. Structurally.

A second position began to form—offset, incomplete.

A branch. Søren stopped. Held.

The second position faded.

The first remained.

That was the final rule.

The system did not prevent divergence. It revealed it.

And once revealed—it would not erase it. Only contain it.

Søren steadied his grip.

This was the moment. Not dramatic. Not visible. But absolute.

He could change it. Or leave it.

And whatever he chose—

would not reset.

Chapter 12: The Cost of Precision

He did not act immediately.

That had not been given to him. It had not been taught in any deliberate way. It had been learned slowly—through repetition, through consequence, through the quiet accumulation of outcomes that did not announce themselves until it was too late to undo them.

The system did not prevent error.

It did not correct it.

It allowed action to complete, and then it preserved the result.

That was how it taught.

Søren held the device steady, the point suspended between it and the platform. The chamber had receded—not vanished, but withdrawn from importance. Its walls, its boundaries, its presence no longer defined the moment.

Everything had narrowed.

Not visually.

Structurally.

The interaction existed within a reduced field:

Him.

The device.

The point.

Everything else persisted only as context.

He shifted his weight slightly.

The movement was controlled, minimal, intentional—but even so, the system registered it completely. The point did not move in space. Instead, its relation to him altered, tightening, relaxing, then tightening again as his position settled.

The adjustment was immediate, precise, and unforgiving.

The system was not tracking where he stood.

It was tracking whether he matched.

Coherence.

Not position.

That distinction had taken too long to understand.

Before, he had tried to align physically—matching angles, distances, measurable coordinates. Now he understood that none of those were primary. What mattered was whether the action and its outcome agreed without contradiction.

Every variable contributed.

The angle of his wrist.

The pressure of his grip.

The timing of movement.

The difference between intention and assumption.

Even that—especially that—carried weight.

He had been here before.

Not as memory.

As outcome.

The structure was familiar, and because of that, so was the failure.

In those earlier sequences, he had not made dramatic errors. Nothing that would have drawn attention in the moment. The deviations had been small—barely perceptible, easy to dismiss.

A fraction too far.

A degree too wide.

A moment too certain.

Each one insignificant in isolation.

Each one preserved.

The system had allowed them all.

It had not resisted.

It had not warned.

It had simply accepted—and retained what followed.

That was the cost.

It did not correct.

It accumulated.

Søren focused—not by concentrating harder, but by removing everything that did not belong to the interaction. The chamber, the descent, the city above—all of it fell away as irrelevant.

Only the alignment remained.

He extended his hand—not toward the point, but around it, defining the space it occupied without collapsing it. The motion was careful, measured against its outcome before it was completed.

The device responded immediately. Its internal geometry shifted in quiet synchronization, and the platform beneath him adjusted in parallel—not reacting, but aligning.

The point remained.

Stable.

Waiting.

He rotated his wrist.

Slowly.

The motion was almost imperceptible, but the system registered it fully. The point did not change form, but its state shifted. A faint extension emerged—not visible as a line, but present as direction.

A suggestion. A path.

He stopped.

Too far. The extension collapsed immediately, returning to singularity without distortion.

He exhaled—not in frustration, but in recalibration.

Precision.

That was the requirement.

Not force. Not intent. Precision.

He adjusted again.

Smaller this time.

Slower.

Reducing the motion to the minimum necessary to test alignment.

The extension formed again.

Held.

Not fully.

But enough.

This time, it did not project outward.

It turned inward.

Into the structure of the platform.

Into the system itself.

Søren felt the shift—not physically, but in how the interaction was defined. The point was no longer separate. It had become a reference within a deeper structure.

That was the distinction.

The change would not occur in the environment.

It would occur in how the system defined it.

He could alter the reference.

Not the object.

That was what he had missed before.

He held the position, allowing the alignment to stabilize without forcing it further. The extension remained—fragile, partial, but present—connecting the point to something deeper within the structure.

Something not visible.

But active.

Søren's grip tightened slightly.

Not from strain.

From awareness.

This was the threshold.

He could complete the extension.

Commit the change.

Or release.

And if he released...

the system would not revert.

It would retain.

He knew that outcome.

He had seen it.

Not in this form, not in this place—but in what followed.

A system that continued.

Mostly.

A city that functioned.

Mostly.

A sequence that held.

Mostly.

Differences too small to disrupt—at first.

A hesitation in timing.

A delay that did not resolve.

A repetition that did not integrate.

Nothing dramatic.

Nothing obvious.

But enough.

Enough to propagate.

That was how errors became reality.

Quietly.

He closed his eyes.

Not to withdraw.

To isolate.

He removed memory.

Removed expectation.

Removed the weight of prior outcomes.

Left only the present interaction.

The point.

The alignment.

Nothing else.

When he opened his eyes, nothing had shifted.

The point held.

The extension remained.

He moved.

Not faster.

More certain.

The alignment completed.

The point did not expand.

It resolved.

The connection to the deeper structure locked into place—not visibly, but with a finality that required no confirmation.

The device responded at once. Its internal geometry settled into a new configuration, the central core clarifying—not brighter, but more exact.

Acceptance.

The platform beneath him stabilized. The subtle variability collapsed into coherence, and the chamber began to return—walls reasserting, distance restoring, the environment regaining relevance.

Søren lowered the device.

The weight had changed.

Not physically.

Resolved.

The point was gone.

Not removed.

Integrated.

He stepped off the platform.

The chamber held steady.

No distortion.

No instability.

That was not reassurance.

It was delay.

He closed the briefcase, the latch sealing with quiet finality. He remained still for a moment, listening—not for sound, but for inconsistency.

There was none.

There never was.

Not immediately.

The system did not reveal consequence.

It distributed it.

Through structure.

Through time. He learned that some conditions must be followed.

He turned toward the steps, then paused once more and looked back at the platform.

Unchanged.

No trace.

No indication of decision.

Only structure.

Søren nodded—not in satisfaction, but in acknowledgment—and began the ascent.

Each step carried him back toward the surface.

Not toward the same city.

Toward a version that would hold what he had done.

Below, the system settled into its new alignment.

Above...

London would begin to reflect it.

Not all at once. Not obviously.

But inevitably.

He did not stop as he moved upward.

But his attention shifted. Not to the city above—but to what had just occurred.

It was no longer enough to observe. The system was consistent. Which meant it could be understood.

He began to order it—not as conclusions, but as constraints.

Alignment did not mean correctness. It meant permission.

The system did not fix what deviated. It preserved it.

Partial actions did not disappear. They remained. And became part of what followed.

Duplication was not repetition. It was conflict. Two states forced into the same structure.

Echo—was something else. Not conflict. Not error.

Memory. Held longer than required.

The system tolerated variation. Until it didn't.

Precision reduced error. But it also reduced tolerance.

Which meant—everything that did not resolve would remain.

That was the cost. Not failure. Accumulation.

He reached the final steps. Light widening above him.

There were others. Not identical. Not repeating.

Resolving. Holding. Failing to do either.

The system was not singular. It was selective.

And whatever lay below—was not where the system began.

It was where it decided.

Søren stepped into the street.

The city received him without interruption.

But the structure had changed. Not outside.

Inside his understanding of it.

And that...

would define what came next.

Chapter 13: The City Adjusts

When Søren emerged, London had not changed.

That was the first indication that it had.

The transition back to the surface offered no resistance—no threshold, no sense of crossing from one condition into another. The city resumed around him as if it had never been interrupted, as if the descent had occurred somewhere outside its structure rather than beneath it.

The air carried the same evening weight. Cool, slightly damp, holding the residue of the day. Traffic moved in familiar patterns, steady and unbroken. Light settled across stone and glass with the same measured consistency he had observed before descending.

Nothing was different.

Everything was adjusted.

Søren stepped onto the pavement and paused—not to orient himself, but to listen. Not for sound. For structure.

The street did not reveal itself immediately. It continued, uninterrupted, offering no obvious signal of change. But as he remained still, allowing the environment to move without his influence, the differences began to emerge.

They were not visible in isolation.

They existed in timing.

A pedestrian crossed at the corner ahead, moving with confidence, neither hurried nor delayed. There was nothing incorrect in the motion, nothing that would draw attention.

And yet, Søren could feel the shift—a fraction of timing, subtle enough to pass unnoticed by anyone not measuring continuity.

Not early.

Not late.

Recalibrated.

A car approached the same intersection and slowed. The adjustment was smooth, almost effortless, but something about it had changed. It was not reacting in the way it would have before.

It was selecting.

The distinction was nearly invisible, but once seen, it could not be ignored.

Søren remained where he was, resisting the impulse to move too quickly through the observation. The system did not reveal itself under pressure. It revealed itself through allowance—when left to operate without interference.

He watched.

Another pedestrian passed behind him, footsteps falling in a steady rhythm. For a moment, the spacing between each step aligned perfectly with the movement of a nearby reflection in a shop window. The synchronization was exact—not approximate, not coincidental.

Too clean.

Then, just as quickly, it dissolved back into ordinary variation.

Søren turned and began to walk.

Not toward a destination.

Not yet.

Observation first.

Confirmation second.

The street carried him forward without resistance. It did not guide him, but it did not oppose him either. The path unfolded naturally, as if the direction he had chosen was already consistent with the system's current state.

He did not question that.

Preference, within the system, was not arbitrary.

It was directional.

As he moved, the adjustments became clearer—not as isolated events, but as part of a larger sequence.

A door closed along the street ahead. The motion completed cleanly, the sound sharp and contained—but the timing lingered just slightly longer than expected, as if the moment had been extended rather than delayed.

The difference was subtle.

But it was intentional.

A conversation between two people walking side by side paused mid-sentence. Not abruptly. Not awkwardly. The pause held just long enough to allow both speakers to recalibrate their rhythm before continuing, each resuming without interruption.

No overlap.

No correction.

Just continuation.

Søren slowed his pace.

Not to examine.

To allow more of the pattern to emerge.

This was not error.

He had seen error before—duplication, misalignment, sequence breaking against itself.

This was something else.

This was correction.

The system was not failing.

It was refining.

He reached the embankment again, the river opening before him as it had earlier—but now the continuity felt different. Not visibly altered, not dramatically changed, but extended in a way that held attention longer than expected.

The Thames moved as before—steady, continuous, indifferent to observation. But its surface now carried light differently. Reflections stretched across the water, holding just slightly longer before breaking, as if the system allowed them to persist beyond their natural limit.

Not frozen.
Not distorted.
Sustained.

Søren rested his hands on the railing. The metal felt cool and familiar beneath his grip, grounding him in something that had not shifted.

He watched.

A boat passed beneath one of the bridges, its movement cutting cleanly through the water. The wake spread outward in predictable arcs, intersecting with the reflections in layered patterns of light and motion.

For a moment, those patterns held.They did not collapse under disruption.

They did not fragment.

They maintained coherence—longer than they should have.

Then, gradually, they released, returning to ordinary motion as if nothing had been extended at all.

Søren nodded once.

The change was holding.

Not forcing.

That distinction mattered more than anything else.

If the system forced alignment, it would fracture under its own constraint.

If it allowed alignment to hold...

it would propagate.

He turned from the river and looked back toward the city.

From this angle, the difference extended further than before. Not visible in any single point, but present in the way sequences connected. Movements aligned more cleanly. Interactions resolved with less friction.

The change had not remained local.

It had begun to spread.

Not evenly.

Not completely.

But enough.

Enough to confirm that the adjustment he had made below had taken root within the structure above.

Søren began walking again.

This time, with direction.

Not imposed.

Chosen.

Toward the square.

Toward the origin.

Chapter 14: The System Responds

Trafalgar Square received him as it had before.

Open. Geometric. Centered.

The symmetry remained intact—not decorative, but structural. The placement of stone, water, and monument aligned with a precision that did not announce itself, yet could not be accidental. Every line resolved into another. Every angle supported a larger coherence that extended beyond what could be seen at once.

And now...

it was aware.

The fountains rose and fell in controlled arcs, water lifting into the evening air before returning to the basin in clean, measured cycles. At first glance, nothing had changed. The motion was consistent, even familiar.

But Søren did not look at the motion.

He listened to the timing.

The intervals between each rise had shifted—not dramatically, not enough to disrupt the pattern—but enough to alter its origin. The rhythm no longer followed a mechanical cycle. It aligned with something internal, something that adjusted in response to the system's state rather than external input.

The square was no longer operating.

It was responding.

Pigeons scattered across the open stone, then returned in loose, shifting clusters. Their movement appeared random, but held a coherence that was difficult to isolate. No single bird led. No pattern repeated. And yet the group moved as if guided by a shared adjustment—each motion independent, but collectively consistent.

Søren stepped into the square.

The stone beneath his feet felt unchanged—solid, familiar, grounded.

The structure did not.

He moved toward the center—not out of instinct, but recognition. The position drew him not by force, but by alignment. As he approached, the space around him tightened—not visibly, but in the way relationships between elements resolved more precisely.

This was a node.

Not the same as the chamber below.

But connected to it.

Above ground, the system did not isolate interaction.

It distributed it.

Søren stopped at the center of the square and remained still.

He did not initiate.

He had learned that much.

Here, the system did not reveal itself through disruption.

It revealed itself through presence.

At the edge of the square...

a figure appeared.

Not entering from a distance.

Not approaching through space.

Resolving into it.

The form gathered from within the structure of the square itself—edges defining, posture stabilizing, presence consolidating until it held fully.

Male.

Defined.

Stable.

Søren did not turn immediately.

He already knew.

Recognition preceded confirmation.

"Earlier than before," the man said.

"Elias Vane."

Søren turned then, the movement controlled and deliberate. No reaction. No surprise. Only acknowledgment.

"You're consistent," Søren said.

Elias inclined his head slightly.

"As are you."

They stood facing each other across a measured distance. The space between them held perfectly—no duplication, no delay, no distortion. The square did not waver under their presence.

This was not a test.

It was an evaluation.

"You completed it," Elias said.

Not a question.

Søren let the moment settle before answering. The system did not require speed. It required accuracy.

"Yes."

Elias studied him—not visually, but structurally. His attention moved across the alignment of the space itself, reading the coherence of the system rather than Søren's expression.

"The extension?" Elias asked.

"Resolved."

A brief pause followed—not hesitation, but verification. The system held. The square did not shift.

Elias nodded once.

"That's new."

"You feel it," Elias said.

"Yes."

"Not in the structure," Elias continued. "In what it no longer allows."

Søren's gaze remained steady.

"It allows less," he said.

"It allows less without breaking," Elias corrected.

A pause.

"That's not the same."

Søren considered.

"No," he said. "It isn't."

Søren's gaze sharpened slightly.

"Not entirely."

Elias allowed the faintest trace of acknowledgment.

"Not entirely," he agreed.

Around them, the square continued its evening rhythm. Pedestrians crossed at its edges. Voices carried and dissolved. Movement continued as if nothing had changed.

But beneath it...

everything had.

"You changed the reference," Elias said.

"You changed what the system measures against," Elias continued.

Søren did not respond immediately.

"It was already measuring," he said.

"Not like this," Elias replied. "Before, it compared. Now it commits."

Søren's expression sharpened.

"Commitment is what prevents drift."

"It's also what prevents recovery," Elias said.

A brief silence.

Søren held his position.

"That depends on whether recovery is necessary."

Elias almost smiled.

"It always is. You just haven't reached the point where you need it."

"Yes."

"And you held it."

"Yes."

Elias exhaled softly—not fatigue, not relief, but consideration.

"That narrows the sequences."

"It doesn't just narrow them," Elias said. "It excludes them."

Søren's gaze shifted slightly.

"Unstable paths should not persist."

"Unstable paths are how the system learns what not to hold," Elias replied.

Søren did not react.

"Learning is not required for stability."

"No," Elias said. "But it's required for survival."

That landed.

Søren held it.

Søren understood immediately. No explanation was necessary.

Fewer possibilities.

More consequence.

"That was the point."

Elias glanced briefly toward the outer edges of the square. Movement continued, but the alignment held tighter than before. Interactions resolved more cleanly. Timing allowed less variation before correcting itself.

The system was holding.

But with less tolerance.

"You've reduced its capacity," Elias said.

"Refined it," Søren replied.

Elias returned his attention to him.

"That's the same thing."

"It isn't," Søren said.

Elias waited.

"Reduction implies removal," Søren continued. "Refinement implies selection."

"And who makes that selection?" Elias asked.

Søren met his gaze.

"The system."

Elias shook his head slightly.

"Not anymore."

A longer pause.

"You crossed that boundary below," Elias said. "You didn't just observe it. You influenced it."

Søren did not deny it.

Søren did not argue.

Because in practice...

it was.

The system now had less room to absorb deviation. Which meant one of two outcomes:

Greater precision.

Or greater failure.

Elias stepped forward.

The distance between them closed cleanly. No resistance. No duplication. The system allowed the movement without adjustment.

"You know what comes next," Elias said.

"It doesn't stop correcting," Søren said. "It stops compensating."

Elias nodded once.

"That's closer."

"Correction implies error," Søren continued. "Compensation implies tolerance."

"And you removed tolerance."

"I reduced it."

Elias exhaled softly.

"That distinction won't matter to the system when it reaches its limit."

Søren held his gaze.

"Say it."

Elias did not hesitate.

"It stops correcting."

"And when it stops," Søren said, "it holds."

Elias studied him.

"For a while," he replied.

Søren's expression did not change.

"And then?"

Elias looked past him—toward the outer edge of the square.

"Then it begins to layer."

Søren understood immediately.

"Accumulation."

"Yes."

"And when accumulation exceeds structure?"

Elias's voice lowered slightly.

"It won't collapse," he said. "It will persist."

Søren's gaze sharpened.

"That's worse."

Elias nodded.

"Yes."

The words settled into the space—not heavy, not dramatic, but absolute.

The square did not react.

The fountains continued their measured rhythm.

The city carried on.

Søren nodded once.

"That was always the direction."

Elias watched him carefully—not for doubt, but for instability.

"And if you're wrong?" he asked.

"I won't be corrected."

Elias held that.

"No," he said. "You won't be."

A pause.

"That doesn't mean the system won't respond."

Søren remained still.

"How?"

Elias's expression shifted—more serious now.

"Not through you."

That mattered.

Søren said nothing.

Elias continued:

"There are others."

Søren's eyes narrowed slightly.

"Not here," Elias said. "Not yet."

Søren did not shift.

Did not look away.

"I won't be corrected."

Silence followed.

Not empty.

Resolved.

The system did not intervene.

Elias stepped back—not retreating, but repositioning within the structure.

"Then this is the last sequence that holds," he said.

"For you," Elias added.

Søren did not respond.

"For this version of alignment," Elias continued.

A pause.

"There are other ways to reach the same structure."

Søren's attention sharpened.

"Not through this system," he said.

Elias shook his head slightly.

"Not through this interpretation of it."

That was different.

Søren held it.

Søren understood.

There would be no further adjustment.

No hidden correction.

No secondary alignment waiting beneath the surface.

Whatever had been set...

would remain.

"You're assuming the system is singular," Elias said.

Søren's gaze did not shift.

"It is."

Elias paused.

"Here."

A longer silence.

"And elsewhere?" Søren asked.

Elias did not answer immediately.

Then...

"It doesn't behave the same way."

That was enough.

Elias turned and walked toward the edge of the square.

His movement remained continuous. No distortion. No fragmentation. No sign of instability.

He did not resolve.

He did not disappear.

He simply left.

Søren remained where he was.

The alignment around him steady.

No fluctuation.

No testing.

The system had shifted again.

Not observing.

Not evaluating.

Holding.

And within that stillness, the implication settled fully—not as a realization, but as a condition:

There would be no further correction.

No second pass.

No hidden tolerance.

What had been set...

would define what followed.

Chapter 15: The Weight of Continuity

Søren did not move immediately.

For the first time since entering London, stillness carried weight—not as the absence of motion, but as the presence of outcome. The system had not paused. It had not slowed. It had committed.

The square held.

The fountains rose and fell in their revised rhythm, each arc completing with a precision that no longer adjusted mid-cycle. There was no correction, no subtle recalibration between movements. What had been set now executed exactly as defined.

Around him, the city moved with quiet consistency. Footsteps crossed the stone in measured intervals. Traffic passed along the perimeter without hesitation or deviation. Voices carried through the open space, overlapping and resolving without interruption.

No distortion.

No duplication.

No visible error.

Which meant there would be no warning.

Søren turned slowly, taking in the full geometry of the square. He was not scanning for anomalies. He was reading structure—how space held movement, how intervals formed between bodies, how timing connected action to response.

Everything aligned.

Every line.

Every distance.

Every sequence.

The placement of people within the square followed a coherence that required no awareness from those participating in it. A man crossed toward the fountain at the exact moment another stepped away, their paths intersecting without friction. A couple paused at the edge of the plaza just long enough for a group behind them to pass before continuing forward.

No hesitation.

No adjustment.

No need.

The system was not correcting.

It was preventing deviation from occurring.

Søren began to walk.

Not toward a destination, but through the structure itself, allowing his movement to intersect with others. Testing—not the presence of alignment, but its limits.

A man approached from his right.

Their trajectories converged at a shallow angle. Under normal conditions, one of them would adjust—slightly, instinctively, without conscious awareness.

Here, neither did.

The spacing between them recalibrated instead. Not visibly, not dramatically, but enough that both paths completed without interference. Søren felt it—the shift in interval rather than direction.

The system had adjusted the relationship, not the individuals.

That was more efficient.

He continued.

A woman stepped from a side street onto the square, her movement integrating instantly into the existing flow. She did not pause to orient herself. She did not hesitate before choosing a direction. The system had already resolved her position before she entered.

Søren slowed.

Not to examine her.

To observe what followed.

Nothing did.

Her presence was absorbed immediately.

No ripple.

No delay.

No visible recalculation.

That meant the system was no longer reacting.

It was anticipating.

He moved toward the edge of the square and stepped onto one of the adjoining streets. The architecture tightened again—buildings closer, movement more constrained—but the alignment persisted without degradation.

It carried.

That was new.

Before, alignment had been local—strong near nodes, weaker at distance. Now, the structure extended outward, maintaining consistency across space without visible decay.

The propagation had not only taken hold.

It had stabilized.

A car turned the corner ahead.

Its motion followed the curve of the street with exact consistency—no hesitation in its trajectory, no variation in speed beyond what was required to complete the turn. The tires traced the arc as if guided by a line already present.

Søren stepped into the road.

Deliberately.

Not to test danger.

To test response.

The car slowed.

Not abruptly.

Not cautiously.

Exactly enough.

The adjustment was so precise it bordered on invisible. There was no excess braking, no margin for error, no allowance for unpredictability.

The system had calculated the interaction fully.

Søren remained in place for a moment longer, then stepped back.

The car resumed immediately.

No correction.

No compensation.

The sequence closed cleanly.

Søren nodded once.

Recognition, not approval.

The system was stable.

But...

it was rigid.

He continued down the street.

The further he moved from the square, the more evident the pattern became. Interactions resolved before they could conflict. Movements aligned before they could diverge. Timing held across multiple layers of activity without breakdown.

It was efficient.

And it was narrowing.

A cyclist passed him on the left, maintaining a steady speed. Ahead, a pedestrian stepped slightly off the curb, then back again—an adjustment so small it would normally go unnoticed.

Here, it resolved perfectly.

No interruption.

No near miss.

No variation.

Søren slowed again.

The system was no longer allowing uncertainty to exist within interactions.

It was eliminating it.

He stopped at a crossing and watched a sequence unfold.

A line of pedestrians moved across the street. A vehicle approached. Under ordinary conditions, there would be a moment of negotiation—a slight hesitation, a misjudged step, a recalibration of pace.

Here, there was none.

Each movement completed exactly once.

No overlap.

No correction.

The crossing resolved with absolute precision.

And for the first time, Søren felt it clearly—not as observation, but as pressure.

The system had removed tolerance.

It had not eliminated error.

It had eliminated the space in which error could be absorbed.

He stepped back from the curb and turned, retracing his path slightly before angling toward another street. The alignment followed him—not reacting, not adjusting, but extending.

That meant the change was no longer confined to nodes or specific conditions.

It had become systemic.

He paused once more and looked back toward Trafalgar Square.

From this distance, nothing appeared different. The space remained open, centered, stable. But he could feel the difference—not in the structure itself, but in how the surrounding movement resolved into it.

The node no longer responded.

It held.

Its function was complete.

Søren exhaled slowly.

The breath felt measured—not forced, not released, but contained within the same structure that governed everything around him.

This was the consequence.

Not failure.

Not success.

Definition.

He lifted the briefcase slightly, adjusting its position in his hand. The motion was small, almost automatic, but the response within him was not.

The weight had changed.

Not physically.

Relationally.

The device no longer belonged to the process.

It belonged to the outcome.

What it carried now could not be undone.

Only extended.

Søren began to walk away from the square.

This time, he did not test.

He did not observe for variation.

The system no longer required analysis.

It required presence.

He moved forward through the city, the patterns holding around him—stable, consistent, precise beyond what natural variation would allow.

And as the distance between him and the square increased, one final realization settled—not suddenly, not imposed, but inevitable:

There would be no further chances to refine.

No second pass.

No hidden correction waiting beneath the surface.

Only the unfolding of what had already been set.

Chapter 16: The Descent Revisited

He did not intend to go back.

That was how he knew he would.

The recognition came without conflict—not as a decision he needed to make, but as something already embedded in the structure of what followed. The path forward had been established. The system held. The city functioned with a clarity it had not possessed before.

And still...

something did not resolve.

Søren continued walking.

The street carried him forward for several blocks, the rhythm of the city settling into a consistency that was almost imperceptible at first. Footsteps aligned without interruption. Conversations began and ended without overlap or hesitation. Vehicles moved through intersections with exact coordination, each motion completing once and only once.

Everything functioned.

Everything resolved.

Nothing required adjustment.

That was the problem.

He slowed.

Not because something had disrupted the system...

but because nothing had.

He stopped at the edge of a crossing and watched as a sequence unfolded in front of him.

A group of pedestrians stepped into the street. A car approached from the right. Under ordinary conditions, there would be a moment of uncertainty—a slight hesitation, a misjudged pace, a subtle recalibration between individuals.

Here, there was none.

Each movement completed exactly once.

No one paused.

No one adjusted.

No one even appeared aware of the others.

And yet the interaction resolved perfectly.

Not through awareness.

Through alignment.

Søren remained still, letting the moment pass without interference.

The system had removed friction.

And in doing so...

it had removed choice.

That realization did not arrive as a thought.

It settled as absence.

The absence of hesitation.

The absence of correction.

The absence of anything that required interpretation.

He stepped back from the curb and continued walking, his pace slower now—not out of caution, but observation. He needed to understand what had been lost, not just what had been gained.

A man exited a building ahead, stepping directly into the path of another pedestrian. There was no glance exchanged, no shift in posture, no visible adjustment.

The space between them changed instead.

Subtly.

Precisely.

Enough to allow both movements to complete without interruption.

Søren watched the exchange from only a few meters away.

Neither man noticed.

Neither needed to.

The system had resolved the interaction before either became aware of it.

He turned down another street.

The same pattern held.

Every movement aligned.

Every sequence completed.

No deviation.

No recovery.

No necessity for either.

He reached a narrow stretch where the buildings pressed closer together, the path constricting just enough that interactions should have required negotiation.

They did not.

A cyclist approached from ahead while two pedestrians moved side by side. Under normal conditions, someone would yield—slightly, instinctively, without conscious thought.

Here, no one did.

The spacing adjusted.

The timing recalibrated.

The sequence resolved without any participant altering their behavior.

Søren stopped.

Watched it happen.

Then watched it happen again.

And again.

Different people.

Same result.

The system had not improved movement.

It had removed variability.

And without variability...

there was nothing left to absorb error.

He exhaled slowly.

The breath felt measured, contained within the same structure that governed everything around him.

A system that no longer required correction was not complete.

It was closed.

That was the distinction.

Before, the system had allowed deviation, then adjusted. It had absorbed error, redistributed it, corrected where necessary.

Now...

it allowed nothing that required correction.

Which meant...

when something did not align...

there would be no recovery.

The thought did not produce urgency.

It produced clarity.

Søren turned.

Not abruptly.

Deliberately.

The motion did not disturb the flow around him. Pedestrians adjusted without awareness. Timing held. Distance recalibrated.

The system allowed the reversal.

And he began walking back the way he had come.

The city did not resist.

It did not guide.

It simply allowed.

That, too, had changed.

Before, movement carried implication—direction shaped by underlying alignment, subtle forces nudging toward interaction points.

Now, direction existed without influence.

The system no longer suggested.

It held.

Søren retraced his path through the streets, the patterns continuing around him with the same quiet precision. The further he walked, the more certain he became.

Nothing would break.

Until it did.

And when it did...

there would be no space left to correct it.

He reached the narrow descent between the buildings.

It appeared exactly as before.

Partially obscured.

Structurally modest.

Easily overlooked.

But now...

it felt different.

Not in form.

In permission.

Before, the descent had carried necessity. The system had required interaction. The space had drawn him inward—not forcefully, but inevitably.

Now...

it offered nothing.

No pull.

No alignment.

No indication that entry mattered.

Søren stood at the threshold and studied it.

The steps descended into shadow, unchanged in geometry, unchanged in spacing, unchanged in surface wear.

Everything identical.

Except the absence of demand.

He stepped forward anyway.

The descent accepted him.

Not with invitation.

With neutrality.

Sound diminished as before—the layered noise of the city thinning, then withdrawing—but not completely. A faint residual continuity remained.

Not sound.

Not light.

Something structural.

Like an echo that refused to fully resolve.

Søren noticed it immediately.

The difference was small.

But definitive.

He continued downward, each step confirming the same condition. The system had not fully separated the layers.

Above and below...

were now connected.

He reached the base.

The chamber opened.

Circular.

Minimal.

Complete.

The platform remained at its center.

Unchanged.

Or...

untouched.

Søren stepped inside.

And waited.

Before, the space had responded to his presence immediately. It had recalibrated around him, redefining position, establishing reference.

Now...

nothing.

No shift.

No adjustment.

No recognition.

He approached the platform and stopped at its edge.

Still nothing.

He stepped onto it.

The silence deepened.

No structural response.

No relational change.

No indication that the system even registered his position.

The platform did not engage.

Søren stood still.

Waited.

Nothing.

The absence was absolute.

He stepped off again.

The chamber remained unchanged—stable, neutral, complete.

The system had not removed the platform.

It had removed access.

He looked down at the faint geometric lines embedded in its surface. They were still there, identical in form.

But inert.

No longer responsive to position.

No longer adjusting to presence.

He set the briefcase down.

Opened it.

The device remained aligned.

Its internal geometry held the configuration he had established earlier. It had not degraded. It had not reset.

It had been preserved exactly as defined.

He lifted it and stepped back onto the platform.

Held it in position.

Waited.

Nothing.

No synchronization.

No resonance.

No shared state.

The connection had been severed.

Not physically.

Functionally.

Søren lowered the device.

Considered.

Not surprised.

Not frustrated.

Confirmed.

This was expected.

Not because the system rejected repetition...

but because it preserved outcome.

The change had been made.

The system would not allow it to be remade.

That was the final constraint.

He closed the briefcase.

The latch sealed with a quiet, contained finality.

He stepped off the platform.

The chamber remained silent.

Complete.

Inactive.

There was nothing more to do here.

There had never been a second attempt.

Only the illusion of one.

Søren turned and began the ascent.

The residual continuity followed him upward—not fully, but enough to confirm what he had already understood.

The system above and below were no longer separate.

They had been unified.

He reached the top of the steps.

The city reassembled around him without transition—sound returning, motion resuming, structure holding exactly as before.

But now he felt it completely.

Not as observation.

As condition.

There would be no return to the moment of choice.

No second alignment.

No correction.

Only consequence.

This was a problem.

Chapter 17: The Vault That No Longer Waits

The city above received him without transition.

There was no shift. No recalibration. No sense of crossing between conditions.

London held.

It did not reassemble around him this time—it had never released him. The continuity he carried upward remained intact, not as something re-established, but as something that had never been interrupted. The boundary between below and above no longer functioned as separation. It had flattened into a single structure, continuous and uninterrupted, as though depth itself had been absorbed into the system's definition.

Søren stepped onto the street and paused.

He listened—not for sound, but for resistance.

The air moved normally. Conversations passed. Footsteps layered across pavement in familiar rhythms. A distant vehicle turned through an intersection. Somewhere behind him, a door closed.

Everything was present. Everything functioned.

But beneath it, nothing pushed back.

No subtle tension beneath the surface. No correction adjusting itself to accommodate him. No shift in timing that acknowledged his presence as a variable within the system.

He stood longer than necessary, waiting—not for change, but for response.

None came.

Nothing moved because he had arrived. Nothing adjusted because he was present.

The system had moved beyond interaction. It had entered execution.

He began to walk, not searching, but confirming.

His steps fell into rhythm with the city without effort. Not because he adapted—but because adaptation was no longer required. The structure accepted him without adjustment, as though his movement had already been accounted for before it occurred.

The alignment persisted across every observable layer—movement, timing, reflection, sequence.

A man crossed the street ahead of him without looking. A car approached and slowed—not abruptly, not cautiously, but with exact timing that required no decision from either participant. The man continued walking. The car continued forward.

No hesitation. No negotiation.

The moment resolved as if it had been written before either of them entered it.

Søren's gaze lingered on the interaction longer than necessary. There had been no risk—not because the participants were aware, but because risk had been removed from the system itself.

He reached the embankment.

The Thames moved steadily below, its surface reflecting the muted sky in long, uninterrupted planes of light. Even disturbance behaved differently now. When a boat passed beneath the bridge, its wake extended outward in widening arcs that intersected with reflected light in clean, geometric patterns. The lines did not break or scatter. They crossed, held, and resolved.

Søren rested his hands lightly against the railing. The metal was cold and solid, unchanged—but the scene below resisted interpretation. Not because it was complex, but because it was too complete.

This was not stability.

It was enforcement.

He turned from the river and moved back into the interior of the city, toward the narrower streets where movement compressed and interactions multiplied. If strain existed, it would not appear in simplicity. It would emerge where complexity demanded flexibility.

The shift was immediate—not in structure, but in density.

Footsteps layered more tightly. Conversations overlapped. Movement required constant adjustment—micro-decisions that had once occurred without awareness.

A cyclist approached from behind as a pedestrian drifted slightly left, narrowing the path. In another moment, one of them would have adjusted. Instead, neither did.

The space between them recalibrated.

The cyclist passed. The pedestrian continued.

No contact. No awareness.

But the distance between them had narrowed beyond what either body should have allowed.

Søren felt it—not as sight, but as tension.

Nearby, a door opened. A man stepped out as another moved in. Their paths intersected at the threshold, close enough that one should have yielded. Neither did. Their movements aligned exactly, each completing once and only once, without hesitation, without deviation.

Everything resolved. Everything held.

Until Søren saw it.

A hesitation.

It was small—almost invisible—but real.

A man walking ahead slowed mid-step. Not because of obstruction, not because of awareness, but because the continuation of his movement did not occur when it should have.

His foot hovered just above the pavement.

For a fraction of a second, his body occupied a position that required completion—and did not receive it.

Then the step landed.

The motion continued.

The sequence resolved.

The man did not react. He did not notice.

Søren stopped.

Not abruptly—but completely.

A woman approached a storefront ahead and reached for the handle. Her hand extended, fingers closing around the metal. The motion was clean, aligned—and then it paused.

Her arm held in place, not by choice, but because something had not yet resolved.

The delay was brief, but not natural. The muscles in her wrist engaged subtly, maintaining position against something unseen.

Then the latch released. The door opened. Her movement continued.

No hesitation. No awareness.

Søren stepped closer.

The structure remained intact. Nothing broke. Nothing misaligned.

But the timing had changed.

It had tightened.

Another instance emerged. Two people walked side by side. One finished speaking. The other turned, ready to respond—and did not.

The pause extended, not as thought, but as delay.

Then the reply came, perfectly formed, precisely placed. The conversation resumed without disruption.

Søren continued walking.

Now he could see it everywhere.

Not failure.

Latency.

Each delay small. Each one absorbed. Each one corrected—for now.

As he moved deeper into the street, the pattern intensified. Interactions overlapped more tightly. Movements required resolution before continuation. Nothing flowed freely anymore.

Everything waited—just long enough—to ensure nothing broke.

Søren exhaled slowly.

The breath did not release cleanly. It lingered—not in his lungs, but in the moment itself.

This was the cost.

Not failure.

Accumulation.

He adjusted the grip on the briefcase. Its weight grounded him—not physically, but structurally. He had removed flexibility. Now the system was enforcing precision against variables that could not be perfectly controlled.

He stopped in the center of the street.

Movement continued around him. People passed. Distances adjusted. Timing held just enough to prevent breakdown.

But beneath it, he could feel it clearly now.

The system was working harder.

Not visibly.

Structurally.

Every interaction required more resolution. More constraint. More control.

He closed his eyes briefly—not to withdraw, but to isolate the pattern without distraction.

Then opened them.

The city continued.

Still aligned. Still functioning.

But no longer effortless.

And the realization settled—not suddenly, not dramatically, but with quiet certainty:

The system would not fail all at once.

It would tighten.

Incrementally.

Until something could no longer align.

And when that happened...

there would be no correction.

Only consequence.

He remained where he was.

Not observing now...

feeling.

The movement around him continued with the same quiet precision, but it no longer passed through him unnoticed. Each step taken nearby registered as a contained event, each motion completing fully before the next could begin. The city did not flow. It advanced.

Søren drew a breath.

It entered cleanly, but did not leave the same way.

There was a delay—not enough to restrict him, not enough to disrupt—but enough that he became aware of the separation between intention and completion. His chest expanded. Held. Then released, the exhale following a fraction behind where it should have been.

He took another breath, slower this time.

The same effect.

Not obstruction.

Offset.

He shifted his weight slightly from one foot to the other.

The transfer did not settle immediately. For a brief moment, both positions seemed to hold at once—the prior stance not fully released, the new one not fully established. His balance remained stable, but the transition carried a subtle resistance, as though the system required confirmation before allowing completion.

Around him, no one reacted.

A woman passed close to his left, her shoulder aligning with his position at a distance that should have required adjustment. It did not. The space between them compressed, held—then released as she moved beyond him. Her pace remained unchanged, but Søren felt the passage as a tightening in the air itself, a brief narrowing of possibility that resolved only after she had cleared it.

Sound began to separate.

Footsteps no longer overlapped naturally. Instead, they arranged themselves in sequence—one landing, completing, then another. The rhythm of the street lost its organic layering and became something more ordered, more discrete.

A voice rose behind him.

"…it won't matter if… "

The sentence stopped.

Not interrupted.

Not cut off.

Held.

Søren turned slightly.

The speaker's mouth remained open at the edge of the unfinished word. The listener faced him, attentive, waiting. The air between them felt stretched—not silent, but suspended.

Then... the sound continued.

"... if the timing stays consistent."

The sentence completed as if nothing had intervened.

Neither man reacted.

They continued walking.

But Søren could still feel the gap where the words had not been allowed to exist.

He looked upward.

Light from a window reflected across the glass of a passing car. The reflection should have shifted continuously as the car moved—but it did not. It held its position along the surface longer than geometry allowed, as though the system delayed its release until the alignment resolved cleanly.

Then it slid forward.

Completed.

Gone.

Søren lowered his gaze.

The pattern was no longer subtle.

It was everywhere.

And it was increasing.

He became aware of his own hands—still at his sides, fingers relaxed. He lifted one slightly, watching the motion not as action, but as sequence.

The movement began.

It continued.

And for the smallest fraction of time...

it did not complete.

His hand remained suspended in transition, neither fully raised nor fully still. The muscles in his forearm engaged to maintain position, holding against something that did not resist physically, but structurally.

Then the motion finished.

His hand settled.

He lowered it again, more slowly.

This time the delay came earlier—closer to initiation. The system was not failing to resolve actions. It was taking longer to confirm them.

Søren's pulse shifted.

Not faster.

More defined.

Each beat distinct, separated by a space that felt slightly extended beyond its natural interval. He placed two fingers lightly against his wrist.

The next beat arrived.

On time...

and not.

There was no irregularity, no arrhythmia, but the perception of timing had changed. Each beat seemed to wait for something before completing, as though the system required alignment even at the level of his own body.

He released his wrist.

This was no longer external.

It was inclusive.

A cyclist approached an intersection ahead.

A car moved toward the same point from the opposite direction.

A pedestrian stepped forward from the curb.

Three trajectories.

Three independent decisions.

In another system, they would negotiate—slow, yield, adjust.

Here...

they did not.

Søren focused.

The cyclist continued at speed. The car did not slow. The pedestrian did not hesitate.

For a moment...

all three occupied positions that could not coexist.

The spacing between them collapsed.

The cyclist's front wheel entered the path of the car. The pedestrian stepped into both.

The moment held.

Not visibly—

structurally.

Søren felt it as pressure behind his eyes, a tightening in his chest, a suspension of breath that was not his own.

Time did not stop.

It refused to resolve.

Then... it did.

The cyclist passed.

The car continued.

The pedestrian reached the opposite side.

No collision. No reaction. No awareness.

But Søren staggered half a step, his balance correcting a fraction too late, his body responding to a strain the others had not felt.

He steadied himself.

The system had held.

But not cleanly.

Not easily.

He could feel where it had stretched.

The delay that followed was longer.

Not seconds.

But longer than before.

A gap where something should have completed—and did not.

Then...

everything resumed. The street continued. Movement restored. Continuity maintained.

But something had changed. The system had required more. And it had taken it.

Søren stood still, breathing carefully now, aware of each inhale as it began, each exhale as it completed—measuring the distance between them, feeling the slight resistance that remained.

This was no longer sustainable.

Not indefinitely.

The tightening would continue. The delays would accumulate. The system would demand greater precision with each interaction, greater control with each resolution.

Until...

He did not need to complete the thought.

He had already seen it.

Not as projection.

As inevitability.

Something would not resolve.

Not because it could not be corrected...

but because the system would not allow imperfection.

And when that moment came...

the failure would not be visible at first.

It would feel like this.

A hesitation.

A delay.

A space where completion should occur...

and does not.

Søren lowered his gaze to the movement around him.

The city remained intact. Ordered. Continuous.

But beneath it, the strain had become undeniable.

He adjusted his grip on the briefcase, grounding himself once more—not in weight, but in cause.

He had done this.

Not by breaking the system.

By perfecting it.

He lifted his head and looked forward.

The street extended ahead, filled with motion that no longer flowed, only resolved.

And somewhere within it...

the first true failure was already forming.

Not visible.

Not yet.

But inevitable.

Chapter 18: The Choice That Echoes

He did not need to search for it.

The next point revealed itself—not through signal, not through instruction, but through alignment. It emerged within the structure of the city the same way everything else now resolved: not discovered, but inevitable.

Not below. Not hidden.

Embedded.

At the end of the street stood a building that did not draw attention to itself. Its design matched everything around it—brick, glass, proportion, spacing—each element consistent with the surrounding architecture. Nothing distinguished it through contrast.

And yet Søren recognized it immediately.

Not because it stood apart...

but because it did not.

Its facade aligned perfectly with the structures beside it. Too perfectly. The spacing between windows resolved with exact precision. The vertical lines held without deviation. Even the subtle irregularities that should have existed—the slight misalignments, the imperfections of construction and time—were absent.

The building did not approximate order.

It completed it.

Søren approached.

His pace did not quicken. It narrowed.

Each step placed with increasing awareness, not of distance, but of relation. The street around him seemed to organize subtly as he moved—not shifting, not adjusting—but confirming his trajectory within it.

The closer he came, the more the surrounding detail faded in significance.

Not visually.

Structurally.

His attention did not wander. It was drawn forward, held in alignment with a point that did not demand recognition, but made all other possibilities less relevant.

He stopped just short of the entrance.

The door was closed. Unmarked. mOrdinary.

A simple surface set within the facade, indistinguishable in material or design from countless others across the city.

And yet...

everything around it converged.

Not loosely. Not approximately. Completely.

Søren let his gaze move across the structure.

The spacing of the windows above. The symmetry of the stone along the frame. The way light reflected across the surface—not scattering, not diffusing, but holding its angles just slightly longer than expected, as though the system delayed release until each reflection resolved cleanly against the geometry.

Even the shadows behaved differently here. They did not soften at the edges or blur with ambient light. They held their boundaries with unusual clarity, contained within the lines that defined them.

Variance had been removed.

What remained was not simply order. It was convergence.

A point not for observation. For action.

Søren stepped forward and placed his hand on the handle.

The metal was cool.

Unchanged.

But his awareness of it was not.

His fingers closed around it, and for a brief moment he felt the same subtle delay he had noticed outside—the separation between intention and completion. The grip formed, but did not fully register until a fraction later, as though the system required confirmation before allowing the contact to exist.

He paused. Not out of hesitation. Recognition. He took a deep breath.

This was not the same as before.

The descent below had defined interaction. The platform there had defined change.

This...

would express it.

He turned the handle. The motion completed cleanly this time. The door opened.

Inside... a room. Minimal. Contained.

The absence of detail was not emptiness. It was intention. No ornament, no excess, nothing to draw focus away from the center.

Where the platform stood.

Søren stepped inside.

The air shifted—not in temperature, not in density—but in behavior. Sound from the street behind him did not fade naturally; it cut off cleanly as the door closed.

Not abruptly. Decisively. The room sealed. The outside world did not disappear. It became irrelevant.

Søren remained still for a moment, allowing his perception to adjust.

His breathing slowed, not by effort, but because the space seemed to regulate it. Each inhale completed fully before the next could begin. Each exhale followed with measured precision. There was no overlap, no irregularity—only sequence.

He became aware of his balance again.

Standing at the threshold, his weight settled evenly between both feet. There was no subtle sway, no unconscious correction. His body held position as if the system itself maintained it, removing the need for continuous adjustment.

He stepped forward.

The platform waited.

Identical in form to the one below.

But not in presence.

The lines embedded in its surface were active—not moving, not shifting, but holding a readiness that extended beyond the physical structure. Søren could feel it before he reached it, a subtle pressure building in the space between himself and the platform, as though interaction had already begun.

He stopped at its edge.

Watched.

The geometry did not search for input.

It responded to his presence.

Waiting.

This was not a point of definition.

It was a point of consequence.

Søren set the briefcase down and opened it.

The latch released with quiet precision.

Inside, the device remained aligned. The configuration he had established below had not degraded. It had persisted exactly as he had left it—stable, coherent, ready.

He lifted it.

The weight felt different here.

Not heavier.

More exact.

As though the mass of it had been fully accounted for within the system, leaving no ambiguity in how it should be held.

He stepped onto the platform. The system engaged immediately.

The room did not vanish. It receded.

Not in distance...

in relevance.

Everything outside the interaction lost priority, fading into a background that still existed but no longer required attention.

The structure narrowed.

Søren felt it physically this time. His peripheral awareness compressed. The sense of space around him tightened—not restricting movement, but reducing unnecessary variation.

The same point appeared.

But altered.

Not singular.

Already extended.

The trajectory he had established before was present—no longer forming, but continuing. It existed not as a potential, but as an active condition within the system.

This was not a new choice.

It was the continuation of the previous one.

Søren held the device steady.

His grip was firm, but not tense. The muscles in his hands engaged just enough to maintain position. He could feel the slight delay again—the separation between adjustment and confirmation—but here it resolved faster, as though the system prioritized this interaction above all others.

The extension pulsed.

Not visually.

Structurally.

He felt it through the device, a subtle instability at its edge. Not failure—lack of completion. A boundary that had not yet been fully defined.

Seeking.

Not direction...

commitment.

Further definition.

Søren's breath slowed again, aligning unconsciously with the rhythm of the system. Each inhale seemed to wait for the pulse to complete before continuing. Each exhale followed only once alignment had been confirmed.

He understood.

The system would not allow reversal.

Only progression.

He could extend it further.

Or hold.

And allow the current state to propagate outward, carrying its consequences into every interaction beyond this point.

His fingers adjusted.

A slight rotation.

A minimal shift in angle.

The response was immediate.

The trajectory extended—just slightly.

Not dramatically.

Precisely.

The change moved outward, not expanding freely, but threading itself into the existing structure, integrating without disruption.

Then...

a second branch began to form.

Søren saw it at the edge of perception—a divergence, subtle but distinct, attempting to establish its own continuity alongside the primary path.

It wavered.

Incomplete.

Unstable.

For a moment, both trajectories existed.

The system strained.

Søren felt it in his grip, a faint resistance building as the device attempted to resolve two outcomes at once.

His pulse shifted again.

Not faster.

Tighter.

The delay between beats shortened, as though the system compressed time within his own body to accommodate the increased demand.

The second branch flickered.

It did not hold.

Søren stopped moving.

Removed variation.

Held position completely.

The instability collapsed.

The secondary path disappeared.

The primary remained.

Stable.

Defined.

Contained.

Søren exhaled slowly.

Not relief.

Recognition.

This was the limit.

For now.

He lowered the device.

The trajectory stabilized further, settling into the structure with a quiet finality that carried no sense of completion—only continuation.

The point did not disappear.

It advanced.

The change moved forward into the system, embedding itself within every layer Søren had already observed.

He stepped off the platform.

The room returned.

Walls regained their presence. Distance reasserted itself. The space expanded outward again, allowing variation back into perception.

His body adjusted—subtly at first. His balance shifted, requiring small corrections that had not been necessary before. His breathing lost its enforced precision, returning to something closer to natural rhythm, though the faint delay remained.

The door stood closed. Unchanged.

He closed the briefcase.

The latch sealed with quiet finality.

Søren remained where he was for a moment.

Not evaluating. Not questioning. Confirming.

The interaction had not ended. It had propagated.

He turned. Opened the door. Stepped back into the street.

The city continued.

Aligned. Precise. Strained.

The patterns held—but now the resistance was unmistakable. Movement resolved, but with effort. Timing remained intact, but no longer freely.

And as Søren walked forward, the realization did not arrive as a thought or conclusion.

It moved with him.

A condition, not an idea.

The choice had not ended.

It had begun to echo. He felt his work was incomplete.

Chapter 19: The Moment Reclaimed

He felt it before he saw it.

Not in the street—but in the interval between steps.

A slight resistance.

Not physical. Not environmental.

Structural yet again.

His foot moved forward, but the completion of the step did not follow cleanly. For a fraction of a second, the motion existed without resolution, his weight suspended between positions that should not coexist. The ground met him—but late. The transfer settled—but not immediately.

He took another step.

The same effect.

Not obstruction.

Interruption.

The rhythm of movement no longer passed cleanly from one moment to the next. Something held between them—not stopping motion, but separating it. Each action completed, but only after a delay that did not belong to him.

Søren slowed.

Then stopped.

The street continued around him.

People moved. Vehicles passed. Doors opened and closed with measured alignment. Conversations formed and completed with the same controlled precision he had already observed.

Everything held.

But beneath that continuity...

something had fractured.

Not visibly.

But present in every transition.

Søren turned.

Midway down the block, a man stood in the same position he had occupied moments earlier.

Not similar.

Identical.

Same posture. Same orientation. The same placement of weight through his legs, the same angle of his shoulders, even the same subtle tension in his hands.

The same moment...

held.

Søren remained still, allowing the scene to unfold.

The man shifted.

Stepped forward.

Merged into the flow of the street exactly as expected—his movement resolving cleanly into the surrounding continuity.

And yet...

a second instance remained behind.

Still.

Unmoving.

Unresolved.

Søren's breath tightened—not in panic, but in precision. He became aware of it again—the delay. The inhale completed, but the exhale held a fraction longer than it should, as though the system required confirmation before allowing it to release.

He stepped closer.

Each step measured.

The first man disappeared into the flow, indistinguishable from everything around him.

The second remained.

A preserved state.

Not fading.

Not dissolving.

Søren stopped two meters away.

The distance did not feel chosen.

It felt defined.

His weight settled—but again, not immediately. For a brief moment, his balance existed between positions before resolving fully, his body correcting subtly for a delay it could not anticipate.

The man did not react.

Did not blink. Did not shift. He did not exist within the current sequence.

He existed within a previous one—now held alongside it.

Søren exhaled slowly.

This was the cost. The system could no longer discard.

It had lost its ability to forget.

He moved to the side, changing his angle of observation.

The figure remained consistent from every perspective. Fabric held its folds exactly. Light reflected across the surface of the man's jacket without variation. Even the minute imperfections—creases, shadows, slight asymmetries—were preserved with absolute fidelity.

Nothing degraded. Nothing approximated.

It was not an echo. It was retention.

Søren became aware of the air between them.

It felt narrower.

Not compressed physically—but defined. As though space itself recognized the boundary between the current sequence and the preserved one, holding them apart with invisible precision.

He raised his hand.

Slowly.

The motion did not complete cleanly. His arm extended—but the final distance held, suspended for a fraction longer than expected. The muscles in his shoulder engaged to maintain position, stabilizing against a delay that had no resistance.

His fingers hovered just short of contact.

The air tightened. Not pushing back. Separating.

A boundary between sequences.

Søren held there for a moment longer, feeling the edge of it—not as surface, but as condition.

Then withdrew.

Understood.

The moment could not be altered.

Only acknowledged.

He stepped back.

As his foot settled, the delay returned—slightly longer this time. His balance corrected, but not immediately, his body adjusting to a timing that no longer aligned with its own expectations.

And as he lifted his gaze...

another instance appeared further down the street.

A woman stood near a doorway. Her hand extended toward the handle. Held. Unresolved.

The fingers curved but did not close. The motion had begun—but had not been allowed to complete.

Søren's focus shifted. Then widened. The pattern was not isolated. It was spreading.

A sound passed behind him—a fragment of conversation.

"…just wait... "

The words held. Not fading. Not continuing.

Suspended in the air as a shape without completion.

Then...

they finished.

"…it will align."

Søren turned his head slightly. The speaker walked on, unaware.

But the gap remained, registered not as silence—but as absence of continuation.

He looked upward.

Light reflected across a window above, but did not move as expected. The reflection held its position longer than geometry allowed, stretching the moment before release.

Then it shifted. Completed. Gone.

Søren lowered his gaze again.

The city extended before him—aligned, precise—

and now layered. He began to walk. Not away. Through.

Each step carried the same delay, now more pronounced. The transfer of weight required correction. His body adjusted continuously, small stabilizing movements emerging where none had been needed before.

He passed the second figure.

It remained. Unaware. Unchanging. And as he moved forward—he began to see more. Subtle at first. A hand held mid-gesture. A step suspended just above the pavement.

A glance paused mid-turn, eyes fixed on something that had already passed.

Each one complete in detail.

Each one incomplete in sequence.

All preserved. All held.

Søren tightened his grip on the briefcase.

The contact grounded him—but even that was no longer immediate. His fingers closed, held, then registered, the sensation arriving a fraction after the action.

The system was no longer selecting a single path.

It was retaining multiple states—without resolving them. He moved past an intersection. Here, the effect intensified.

Three preserved instances occupied the same space—a cyclist mid-turn, a pedestrian mid-step, a vehicle just entering the frame of motion.

All held. All coexisting.

For a moment, Søren felt it—not as sight—as pressure.

A compression of possibility, where too many outcomes existed without resolution.

His vision tightened.

Not blurred—focused too precisely. Each detail sharpened beyond comfort, as though the system attempted to maintain clarity across overlapping states.

His breath caught. Held. Released—late. He slowed again.

Not stopping—but reducing movement to maintain control over his own timing.

This was not collapse.

Not yet.

The system still held alignment. Still maintained structure. But it no longer reduced. It no longer chose. It retained. Accumulated. Layered. Continuity was becoming density.

Søren adjusted his grip on the briefcase yet again, feeling the delay in contact, the slight misalignment between action and confirmation.

He did not resist it.

He accounted for it.

Measured his movement against it.

And as he continued forward, stepping carefully through a city that now existed in overlapping states...

the realization did not arrive as a conclusion.

It was already present.

This was not failure.

It was overflow.

Chapter 20: The Argument That Defines Time

He found Elias where the structure was most strained—not in a square, not in an open space, but in a corridor between buildings where movement compressed and interactions overlapped, forcing the system to reconcile multiple variables within limited space.

The corridor narrowed the flow into something controlled and exact. People passed within inches of one another, shoulders nearly touching, trajectories intersecting at angles that should have required constant adjustment. Instead, movement resolved with forced precision. Søren felt it immediately—the slight delay in each step, the subtle correction in his balance as his weight transferred just a fraction later than expected.

Elias stood still. Not resolved, not duplicated—anchored.

The difference was immediate and unmistakable. Where others seemed to move through resistance, Elias existed within it without distortion. The air around him tightened, but did not layer. The system held him differently.

Søren approached and stopped within three meters.

The distance settled into place as if defined externally. Søren felt his stance adjust—not consciously, but in response to a timing that no longer aligned perfectly with his own body. His breath entered cleanly, but the exhale followed a fraction late, held for an instant too long before release.

"You see it," Søren said.

The words left him with slight delay at their edges, the final sound completing just after it should have, as though the system required confirmation before allowing them to resolve.

Elias nodded once. "I always did."

His voice carried without interruption. Where surrounding sounds seemed to fragment or hold between beats, Elias's words moved cleanly from beginning to end.

Søren's gaze moved briefly past him, tracing the layered moments accumulating along the edges of the street—subtle distortions of continuity now held in place.

A hand remained suspended near a doorway. A step hovered just above the pavement further down. Light held along the edge of a window, refusing to shift until the geometry resolved.

"You didn't stop it."

"I couldn't."

"You chose not to."

Elias met his eyes. "I chose to allow correction."

As he spoke, Søren became aware of the space between them tightening again—not physically, but structurally. The air felt more defined, as though the system was constraining the interaction to maintain clarity.

Søren shook his head slightly.

The motion completed, but not immediately. His head turned, held, then settled—his body compensating subtly for a delay that no longer surprised him.

"There is no correction. Only preservation."

"Not exactly," Elias said.

Søren's gaze held.

"Correction still exists," Elias continued. "You've just displaced it."

"Into what?" Søren asked.

Elias did not hesitate.

"Into time itself."

A pause.

Søren frowned slightly.

"That's not a mechanism."

"No," Elias said. "It's a constraint field."

Søren absorbed that.

"You're suggesting time behaves as a bounded state system."

"It always has," Elias replied. "You've just collapsed its degrees of freedom."

Elias stepped forward. The space between them tightened, but did not fracture, did not duplicate.

Behind Elias, a passerby moved between two preserved figures, threading through positions that should not have allowed passage. The moment held, then released, the system forcing continuity forward.

"Not before," Elias said.

"Before was tolerance," Søren replied. "Not correction."

"Tolerance wasn't weakness," Elias said. "It was entropy management."

Søren's expression sharpened.

"Entropy is loss."

"Entropy is flexibility," Elias corrected. "Loss only occurs when the system refuses to redistribute it."

Søren considered that.

"You're saying I removed entropy."

"You localized it," Elias replied. "Now it has nowhere to go."

That landed.

The city continued around them—movement threading between held moments, continuity forced through increasing density.

A fragment of sound passed behind Søren—footsteps landing in sequence rather than overlap. One step completed before the next began, the rhythm no longer fluid but ordered.

Elias gestured subtly toward the street. "This is your precision."

Søren did not look. "I removed instability."

Elias held his gaze. "You removed release."

"And with it," Elias continued, "you removed temporal decay."

Søren's eyes narrowed slightly.

"Decay is inefficiency."

"No," Elias said. "Decay is resolution."

A pause.

"Without decay," Elias added, "states don't collapse. They persist."

Søren looked past him briefly—at the layered figures.

"I've stabilized them."

"You've prevented them from resolving."

That distinction mattered.

The words settled between them—not sharp, not loud, but final.

Søren felt them more than heard them. His breath entered again, but held briefly before release, the delay now consistent enough to measure.

Søren considered them. Then, without resistance... "Yes."

Elias exhaled. "That's the same thing."

His breath moved cleanly. Søren's did not.

Søren did not argue. Because now, it was.

The system had relied on release to maintain continuity. The ability to discard—to let moments pass without consequence—had allowed alignment to hold despite imperfection. Now everything remained. Every deviation. Every partial alignment. Every unresolved interaction.

Accumulating.

Søren's grip tightened slightly on the briefcase. The contact registered just after the action, his fingers closing before the sensation fully arrived.

Elias stepped closer.

"You've turned time into structure."

"You've discretized it," Elias said.

Søren shifted slightly.

"Time isn't discrete."

"It is now," Elias replied. "You've quantized continuity."

Søren's mind tracked that instantly.

"Then transitions become state changes."

"Yes."

"And unresolved states... "

"... don't disappear," Elias said. "They accumulate as parallel configurations."

Søren exhaled slowly.

"That's not sustainable."

"No," Elias said. "It's not designed to be."

Søren's expression remained steady. "It always was."

"Not like this."

Søren lifted the briefcase slightly, feeling its weight—not physical, but conceptual.

Even the lift carried a subtle delay, the upward motion completing before the full sense of weight settled into his arm.

"Now it's visible."

Elias studied him. "And what happens when it fills?"

"It doesn't fill like a container," Elias said.

Søren waited.

"It saturates like a field."

That was different.

"Define saturation," Søren said.

Elias gestured toward the street.

"When every possible resolution occupies the same interval," he said, "and none can collapse without displacing another."

Søren's grip tightened.

"Then continuity stops."

Elias shook his head.

"No."

A pause.

"It fragments into competing continuities."

That was worse.

Søren did not answer immediately.

Because he could feel it now—not just in the environment, but within the interaction itself. The pressure of accumulated states, the density of unresolved moments pressing against continuity.

His pulse remained steady—but distinct. Each beat separated by a space that felt slightly extended beyond its natural rhythm.

But he understood the direction.

"It won't."

"You're assuming linear progression," Elias said.

Søren's gaze sharpened.

"That's the only model that holds."

"Not everywhere," Elias replied.

A beat.

"There are systems that branch instead of resolve."

Søren stilled.

"Not this one."

Elias met his gaze.

"Not yet."

Elias's expression sharpened. "That's not an answer."

"It's a condition."

Silence settled between them as the system strained subtly around their position—movement threading through preserved moments with increasing effort, continuity no longer effortless but enforced.

A figure behind Elias remained mid-turn, eyes fixed in a direction that no longer existed. A door nearby held halfway open, its motion paused between states.

Elias shook his head. "You're still assuming it can hold."

"It doesn't need to hold everything," Søren said.

"It does now," Elias replied.

Søren said nothing.

"You removed selection," Elias continued. "Now retention is the default."

Søren's expression tightened slightly.

"Then selection has to be reintroduced." "This has possibilities."

Elias watched him carefully.

"Yes."

A pause.

"But not the way you think."

Søren met his gaze. "It has to."

Elias stepped back—not retreating, but creating space.

The separation introduced a brief tension in the air, as though the system needed to recalibrate the interaction across a larger distance.

"For what?" "Continuity."

"Continuity isn't survival," Elias said.

Søren didn't respond.

"It's persistence," Elias continued. "Survival requires adaptation."

Søren met his gaze.

"And adaptation requires release."

Elias nodded once.

"Now you're close."

Elias almost smiled. "That's what it had before."

"It had something else," Elias said.

Søren waited.

"Choice."

A pause.

"You've reduced choice to outcome."

Søren considered that.

"Outcome is the point."

"Outcome is the result," Elias corrected. "Choice is the system."

That reframed everything.

Søren did not respond.

Because that was the argument.

Not about what the system was—but what it should be.

Elias turned, looking out across the layered city, where accumulation was no longer theoretical but visible.

A cyclist remained suspended mid-turn. A conversation lingered between words. Light held along the edge of glass, refusing to complete its shift.

Then back at Søren.

"You've defined it."

"You've defined one behavior," Elias continued.

Søren didn't respond.

"Not the system," Elias said.

A pause.

"There are other implementations."

Søren's attention sharpened.

"Where?"

Elias didn't answer immediately.

Then...

"Different environments."

Another pause.

"Different densities."

Søren held that.

"And different observers."

"Yes."

"And now it defines you."

Søren felt the truth of that—not as realization, but as condition. His timing, his perception, even his breath had been drawn into alignment with the system he had created.

Søren did not deny it.

Elias nodded once. "Then we're done here."

"You think you're alone in this," Elias said.

Søren didn't respond.

"You're not."

A beat.

"Others won't approach it the way you did."

Søren's gaze didn't shift.

"They won't need to."

That mattered.

"How?" Søren asked.

Elias turned slightly.

"They'll inherit your constraints." "That is an important understanding."

A longer pause.

"And challenge them."

He stepped away. This time, he did not hold. He moved—integrating into the flow of the city without resistance.

Søren watched closely.

No duplication. No preservation. No delay.

Elias moved cleanly through continuity. Different.

Søren remained where he was. The argument unresolved. The system continuing. He drew a breath.

Held.

Released... late.

And the accumulation... still increasing.

Chapter 21: The Edge of Holding

It did not break. It thickened.

The change was not sudden. It did not arrive as rupture or visible failure. It accumulated—quietly, steadily—until the space Søren moved through no longer behaved as it had moments before.

The air itself seemed to carry definition now. Not resistance, not obstruction—but presence. Each step he took met the ground cleanly, but the transfer of weight settled with a faint delay, his body adjusting continuously to maintain alignment.

Søren walked through the city as the layers increased—not rapidly, not dramatically, but steadily. Each preserved moment added density, each unresolved state occupying space that could no longer be released.

He became aware of his breathing again.

Inhale—complete. Exhale—held. Released—late.

At first, the effect was subtle.

Then it wasn't.

A narrow street became difficult to navigate—not because of crowding, but because of presence. Moments held in place forced current movement to adjust around them, creating paths that had never existed before.

Søren adjusted his own path carefully, deliberately—placing each step between preserved instances, timing each turn to avoid a held gesture.

A hand remained extended at shoulder height near a doorway. Søren angled slightly to pass beneath it, the distance exact, his movement aligning with a space that had not been designed for passage.

He moved through it.

But the effort increased.

His balance required constant correction now. Each shift of weight completed—but only after a subtle delay, forcing his body to compensate for timing that no longer aligned with instinct. His stride shortened, not by choice, but by necessity.

Sound behaved differently here.

Footsteps no longer blended into ambient rhythm. They arrived in sequence—one completing, then another—each occupying its own defined interval. Voices carried, but with gaps between phrases that did not belong to thought or hesitation.

He reached an intersection and stopped.

Watched.

The pause settled into him with unusual clarity. His body held position—but not effortlessly. Small stabilizing adjustments emerged in his stance, muscles engaging where they had once remained passive.

Traffic flowed. Pedestrians crossed. And within it—layers.

A car paused mid-turn, held in place, while another completed the same motion in the present sequence. The preserved vehicle remained angled into the intersection, its reflection fixed along the surface of a nearby window.

A cyclist leaned into a curve—preserved—while a second passed through the same space moments later, the two trajectories occupying the same geometry without interaction.

A pedestrian stepped forward—completed—while another instance of that same step remained suspended just behind, weight forward, never landing.

The system was accommodating. But not efficiently.

Accommodation without release was unsustainable.

The system was performing forced resolution—recalculating paths in real time without reducing state load.

That meant one thing:

No decay.

No temporal dissipation.

Every state persisted.

Søren adjusted his step again.

The delay increased.

Not random.

Cumulative.

Søren exhaled slowly.

The breath caught slightly at its release, the delay now long enough that he had to account for it consciously.

This was the edge.

Not collapse. Not yet.

A threshold condition.

The system had entered a constrained phase space—too many valid states occupying a limited structural interval.

Søren tracked it immediately.

This was no longer linear progression.

It was density-driven interaction.

Each preserved moment was not just retained—it was competing for resolution.

Not collapse. Not failure. Capacity.

He stepped into the intersection.

Immediately, the system responded.

Movement adjusted around him—not smoothly, but precisely. Too precisely. Every path recalculated, every interaction resolved with exact timing that left no margin for variation.

A vehicle approached, its trajectory shifting just enough to pass without contact. The adjustment was mathematically perfect—but physically improbable, the spacing narrowing beyond what should have allowed safe passage.

A pedestrian crossed in front of him, threading between two preserved figures, their body passing through a space that existed only because the system had forced it to.

Søren felt it. Not as sight—as pressure.

This was not spatial compression.

It was state overlap.

Multiple valid outcomes occupying the same coordinate in time.

The system had lost its ability to collapse probability into singularity.

Instead...

it retained all viable states.

Søren exhaled slowly.

That was the failure condition.

Not collapse.

Indecision.

A compression of possibility, where too many states occupied the same structure.

His step forward delayed—just slightly. His body held between positions for a fraction longer than expected before settling fully into motion.

No margin. No tolerance.

He evaluated options.

Not actions—constraints.

Increasing precision further would collapse movement entirely.

Reducing alignment would destabilize continuity.

Neither held.

A third condition was required.

Not control.

Not release alone.

Selective release.

But the system no longer supported selection.

Not directly.

He crossed to the far side.

Turned. Looked back.

The rotation completed—but again, not cleanly. His vision shifted, then settled, the final alignment arriving just after the motion itself.

The intersection held.

For now.

That qualifier mattered.

The system could maintain forced continuity only while the number of active states remained below saturation.

Once exceeded...

resolution would require displacement.

Or redefinition.

Søren's mind moved ahead. Displacement would break continuity. Redefinition would change the system.

But the density had increased again.

A second preserved vehicle now occupied the same turn. A fragment of conversation lingered mid-air near the crossing, words held between speakers before resolving.

Søren lifted his gaze.

The city extended outward—layered, precise, and increasingly full.

The effect was no longer isolated to confined spaces. It spread across the visible structure, moments accumulating along edges, within movement, across every interaction.

He became aware of his grip on the briefcase. His fingers tightened. Held. Then registered. The sensation arrived just after the action.

He understood now. He had not removed instability. He had converted it. From dynamic variation—to static accumulation.

The system had always contained error. Now it preserved it.

That distinction would define everything that followed.

The system would not fail suddenly.

It would reach a point...

where no new moment could be absorbed without displacing another.

He felt that limit not as abstraction, but as approaching condition. The delays had lengthened. The density had increased. The effort required for each interaction had grown.

And when that happened...

something would have to give.

He evaluated the possibilities.

Not in sequence... but in structure.

Option one: Force collapse. Eliminate competing states. Immediate continuity. Irreversible loss.

Option two: Allow saturation. Maintain all states. Continuity degrades into density. Eventual fragmentation.

Option three...

He stopped there. Not yet. Not by choice. By necessity.

Søren remained still for a moment longer, allowing his breathing to settle into the altered rhythm—measured, delayed, controlled.

Then he turned and began walking again, the briefcase steady at his side.

Each step now placed with intention.

The system could not be forced back.

It could only be reconditioned.

Constraints had to change.

Not globally.

Locally.

At the point of highest pressure.

Søren adjusted his path again.

Not avoiding the density.

Moving through it.

Measuring.

Each movement accounted for.

The system held. The layers built. And somewhere ahead...

he could feel it now, not as distance, but as inevitability...

the limit was waiting.

Not as failure.

As transition.

The system would not break.

It would evolve...

or fragment into parallel continuities.

Søren did not yet know which.

But he understood this:

Whatever he chose next

would not correct the system.

It would define it.

Chapter 22: The One Who Stayed

He recognized the place before he saw it.

Not by structure—but by absence.

The shift registered first as relief—not emotional, not conscious, but physical. As Søren moved through the street, the subtle resistance he had been compensating for began to ease. His steps settled more cleanly. The delay between movement and completion shortened, not entirely gone—but reduced.

The city had been growing dense, layered with held moments, each preserved state occupying space within the system's tightening framework. Movement had become precise, calculated, constrained.

Here, it opened. Not wide. Not empty. Clear.

The transition was immediate once he crossed the threshold. The pressure that had defined the surrounding streets did not follow him inside. The air did not tighten. The space did not demand correction.

A narrow courtyard between buildings, partially obscured from the street, where the density thinned and the layers receded. The alignment remained—but the accumulation had paused.

Søren stepped inside and stopped. His weight settled fully this time.

Not instantly—but without resistance. His balance required no correction. His breathing shifted again—inhale, exhale—both completing within the same moment, no delay separating them.

The space held a different quality. Not less precise—more selective.

Only one sequence remained active here.

No preserved gestures. No layered positions. No overlapping states.

Just continuity.

Søren became aware of the difference not as absence—but as permission. Movement could complete without confirmation. Time passed without being held.

He exhaled slowly. So—there were places where the system had chosen to retain singularity. Not everywhere. But somewhere.

The realization settled into him with unusual clarity. Not as conclusion—but as contrast. The system had not fully collapsed into accumulation. It had not entirely lost the ability to release.

It had confined it.

He moved further in.

Each step required less adjustment now. The subtle corrections his body had been making without awareness were no longer necessary. His stride lengthened slightly—not by decision, but because it could.

At the far end of the courtyard, a figure stood still, facing him.

Not resolving. Not duplicating.

Holding.

The presence was immediate—not because of movement, but because of stability. Where everything beyond the courtyard existed in layered states, this figure occupied a single one completely.

Søren slowed, then stopped three meters away.

The distance settled naturally this time. No external definition. No imposed alignment.

The figure did not move. Did not shift. Did not waver.

His posture remained consistent—not preserved, not frozen—but actively held, as though continuity here required no correction.

"You stayed," Søren said.

His voice carried cleanly. No delay at the edges. No fragmentation in sound.

The man nodded once. "Yes."

His voice was steady. Grounded. Present.

Not like the others. Not placed. Not partial. Søren studied him.

The face was clear, defined—no ambiguity, no unresolved structure. Light moved across it normally, not held, not delayed. The smallest movements—the rise and fall of breath, the subtle tension of muscle—completed without interruption.

"You're not part of the accumulation," Søren said.

"No."

"How?"

A pause.

But this pause was different.

Not held.

Not delayed.

Chosen.

Then... "I chose before you did."

"You chose to stop," Søren said.

"Yes."

"Before refinement."

"Yes."

"Before constraint."

The man nodded once.

"Before collapse into structure."

Søren's gaze sharpened.

"You're saying the system was still dissipative."

"It could still release," the man replied.

A pause.

"It could still forget."

The words settled.

Søren's gaze sharpened.

"That's not possible."

"It is here."

Søren considered.

Not reacting.

Measuring.

Then... "You didn't refine."

"No."

"You held."

"I didn't hold everything," the man said.

Søren watched him.

"I held only what completed," he continued.

"And the rest?" Søren asked.

"Passed."

Søren's expression tightened slightly.

"You allowed loss."

"I allowed resolution."

That distinction mattered.

"Yes."

Søren understood.

Not completely—but enough.

The man had not engaged the system's precision. Had not extended the trajectory. Had not reduced tolerance.

He had stopped.

At a point where continuity still allowed release.

Søren became aware of his own state again—of the alignment he carried, of the subtle delay that still lingered within him even here. The courtyard reduced it—but did not remove it.

"You accepted variation," Søren said.

"Yes."

"And the system kept you."

The man shook his head slightly.

"I kept the system."

"You maintained entropy flow," Søren said.

The man considered the phrasing.

"Yes."

Søren nodded slightly.

"You preserved temporal decay."

"I preserved continuity."

Søren exhaled slowly.

"They're not the same."

"No," the man said. "But one requires the other."

Silence settled between them.

And again, this silence was not held—it passed.

The courtyard remained clear—no layers forming, no preserved states accumulating.

Just flow.

Søren felt the difference immediately.

The absence of density.

The absence of strain.

The absence of weight.

His breath moved freely now. His balance required no correction. Even his grip on the briefcase registered fully at the moment of contact, not after.

But the contrast made something else clear...

this state was not dominant.

It was contained.

"You're outside it," Søren said.

"No," the man replied. "I'm within it... before it closes."

"You exist at an earlier state boundary," Søren said.

The man didn't respond immediately.

Then...

"Yes."

"Pre-saturation," Søren continued.

"Pre-constraint lock," the man said.

Søren's eyes narrowed slightly.

"And after?"

The man held his gaze.

"There is no after for this state."

The words introduced a boundary—not spatial, but temporal.

Søren stepped closer. Two meters now.

The space did not tighten. Did not adjust.

It simply held.

No pressure.

No correction.

"What happens when it fills?" Søren asked.

The man met his gaze.

"It doesn't."

Søren frowned slightly.

The motion completed cleanly—no delay, no correction.

"It already is."

The man shook his head.

"What you're seeing isn't fullness," he said. "It's refusal."

"Refusal to release," Søren said.

"Yes."

"Refusal to collapse state."

"Yes."

"Refusal to choose."

The man's expression shifted—slightly.

"That's closer."

A pause.

"The system is not overloaded," he said. "It's undecided."

Søren absorbed that immediately. He did not respond immediately.

Because that reframed everything.

Not accumulation as limit.

Accumulation as consequence.

"The system isn't failing," the man continued. "It's holding what you won't release."

Søren's grip tightened on the briefcase.

This time, the sensation matched the action perfectly.

"I removed instability."

"You removed forgetting."

"Forgetting is not loss," the man continued.

Søren remained still.

"It is selection."

A longer pause.

"You removed the system's ability to discard non-essential states."

Søren's grip tightened.

"That was necessary for precision."

"It was necessary for control," the man replied.

Another pause.

"But not for continuity."

The words landed.

Not new.

But clearer. Sharper.

More precise than Elias had framed them.

Søren glanced briefly toward the entrance of the courtyard—toward the layered city beyond.

From here, the density was visible again. Preserved figures at the edge of motion. Delayed reflections. Paths that forced themselves through accumulated states.

Then back.

"If I restore it... " he began.

"You can't," the man said.

Søren stopped.

"Why not?"

"Because you didn't change the system," the man replied.

A pause.

Then... "You changed its condition."

"You shifted it from dynamic to static equilibrium," the man said.

Søren considered.

"That implies reversibility."

The man shook his head.

"No."

A pause.

"Dynamic systems can recover."

"And static ones?"

"They persist."

That landed.

Søren understood.

Not a setting.

A state.

And states did not revert.

"You cannot return to a prior state space," the man continued.

Søren didn't respond.

"You can only transition into a new one."

A pause.

"And each transition reduces available pathways."

Søren's gaze sharpened.

"So eventual convergence is inevitable."

The man shook his head slightly.

"Not convergence."

A beat.

"Constraint."

They evolved.

The realization settled fully now—not as theory, but as limitation. The system could not be returned to what it had been.

Only moved forward.

He stepped back slightly.

The courtyard remained stable.

Unaffected.

"You're not part of what comes next," Søren said.

"You could have been," Søren said.

The man met his gaze.

"Yes."

"Why didn't you continue?"

A longer pause. Not delayed. Considered.

"Because continuation requires compromise."

Søren said nothing.

"And compromise accumulates," the man continued.

Søren understood that. Too well.

The man nodded once.

"No."

"Then what are you?"

A faint shift in expression. Not quite a smile.Not quite anything.

"I'm what remains," he said.

"You're a reference state," Søren said.

"Yes."

"Outside progression."

"Yes."

"But still within the system."

The man nodded.

"I define what was possible before you changed it."

A pause.

"And after?" Søren asked.

The man did not answer immediately.

Then...

"That's not mine to define."

Søren held his gaze.

"There will be others," the man said.

Søren stopped. Not turning.

"Not like me," the man continued.

Søren waited.

"And not like you."

A pause.

"They won't begin where you did."

Søren's grip tightened slightly.

"Why?"

The answer came cleanly.

"Because you removed that path."

A longer silence.

"And what replaces it?" Søren asked.

The man's voice lowered slightly.

"Something that doesn't resolve the same way."

Then turned.

As he moved toward the exit, he felt it again—the subtle return of delay, the faint resistance beginning to re-enter his movement even before he fully left the courtyard.

Behind him, the space remained clear.

Ahead, the density waited. The courtyard stayed clear behind him. The city waited ahead.

And the distinction settled with quiet certainty:
There were those who moved forward within the system...
and those who had chosen not to.

He realized critical system truths:
forgetting equaled selection,
accumulation equaled unresolved persistence,
static systems don't fail—they persist,
evolution did not equal recovery.

Now he understood. He didn't break the system.

He changed its phase.

Chapter 23: The Second Choice

He did not need to search for it.
The next point revealed itself through pressure.
Not visible.
Felt.

The sensation began before the location clarified. Søren became aware of it in the same way he had begun to perceive the system's strain—through subtle misalignments in his own body. His step shortened without intention. The transfer of weight from heel to toe did not complete cleanly, as though the space ahead resisted resolution.

His breath followed. Inhale—complete. Exhale—held. Released—late.

Something ahead was no longer absorbing the system's accumulation.

The city had thickened further—layers accumulating, preserved moments increasing, movement threading through increasingly constrained space.

And within that...
a point of resistance.

The closer he moved, the more pronounced the effect became. Sound narrowed into sequence—one footstep landing, then another—no longer overlapping. Light held against surfaces longer than it should, reflections lingering as though waiting for permission to shift.

The pressure gathered.

Not pushing outward...

holding inward.

Søren moved toward it.

Each step more deliberate than before. Each interaction requiring calculation. His body adjusted continuously—small corrections in balance, subtle shifts in posture—compensating for a timing that no longer aligned naturally with movement.

The system was still holding.
But barely.

He reached the edge of a narrow street and stopped.

At its center...
a convergence.

Not of structure.
Of accumulation.

The space did not appear different at first glance. Buildings remained aligned. The street retained its form. But within that form...

too much occupied too little.

Multiple preserved moments overlapping within the same spatial interval.

A hand mid-motion. A step mid-stride. A turning head.
All occupying the same point.
Not merging.
Not resolving.
Holding.

Søren's vision tightened as he focused.

The overlapping states did not blur into one another. Each remained distinct, defined, complete in its own frame—yet all present within the same volume of space. The system had retained each one without selecting between them.

Søren approached slowly.

The air itself felt denser here—not physically, but relationally. The space between positions no longer belonged to a single sequence. It had been divided, layered, compressed.

As he stepped closer, his movement lagged again—his foot descending, holding for a fraction longer than expected before making contact. His balance corrected a moment late, his body adjusting to a timing that no longer predicted outcome.

The system was allocating multiple states to the same space without releasing any.

This was the limit.
Not reached.
Approaching.

He set the briefcase down and opened it.

The motion completed, but the sensation followed after—a familiar delay that had now become constant. The latch released. The lid lifted.

Inside, the device remained aligned.

Stable.

Ready.

But even here, Søren sensed the difference. The device no longer existed outside the system's strain. Its presence was part of it—its geometry subtly responsive to the pressure building around them.

He lifted it and stepped forward...
into the convergence.

The transition was immediate.

The system reacted.

Not with duplication.
With strain.

The air tightened sharply—not resisting him, but defining him within multiple overlapping conditions. Søren felt it in his chest first—a compression that was not physical, but structural, as though his breath itself had to align with more than one sequence at once.

The layers pressed inward, multiple preserved states tightening around the active sequence.

For a moment, Søren experienced it directly.

Not as observation...

as inclusion.

His hand holding the device existed in more than one position—not visibly, but perceptually. The motion of his grip felt extended, as though the action had not yet fully resolved into a single outcome.

The device responded.

Its internal geometry shifting rapidly—not seeking alignment, but accommodating.

Søren watched the subtle changes—not visually distinct, but felt through the way the device resisted and accepted pressure at the same time.

It was no longer refining.

It was compensating.

Søren held it steady.

The convergence pulsed—not visually, but structurally.

Each pulse corresponded with a slight tightening in the space around him, a moment where resolution was attempted—but not completed.

The system was attempting to resolve...
without release.

Resolution required collapse.

Collapse required selection.

The system no longer supported either.

Søren held the device steady. This was not a failure of structure.

It was a failure of constraint. He understood that constraint must change.

He understood.

This was the second choice.

Not a reversal.

A redefinition.

The first choice had narrowed the system...

reduced its tolerance, forced alignment, preserved state.

This...

would change how it allowed resolution.

Not to extend. Not to define further. To allow.

Søren adjusted his grip. Not tightening. Relaxing.

The motion was deliberate. His fingers eased their hold, reducing precision rather than increasing it.

The effect was immediate—but subtle.

The device responded. Not as a tool executing instruction—but as a system translating constraint into behavior. Not as control—but as mediation.

Its internal geometry softened—not losing structure, but expanding tolerance.

The rigid alignment that had defined its behavior loosened. Not collapsing—but permitting variation within its form.

The convergence shifted.

Not collapsing. Loosening.

Søren felt the difference first in his own body.

The pressure eased slightly. His breath completed more cleanly. The delay between inhale and exhale shortened—not eliminated, but reduced.

One of the preserved moments faded.

It did not vanish abruptly.

It thinned.

Its presence diminished until it no longer occupied the same relational space.

Not erased.

Released.

The space adjusted.

The remaining states shifted subtly—not expanding, but redistributing. The compression lessened.

Søren exhaled.

There.

That was it.

Not precision. Permission.

Precision constrained outcome.

Permission constrained behavior.

That distinction mattered.

Søren was no longer defining what the system should become...

only what it must allow.

He held the position.

The device continued to adjust.

The system adapted.

Not by correcting...

by redistributing.

The preserved states did not disappear.

They were no longer required to remain.

That was enough.

Another moment released. Then another. And then again another.

Each one following the same pattern—presence softening, thinning, then passing—not removed, but no longer retained.

Not all.

Not at once.

But enough.

The density decreased.

Søren became aware of his own balance stabilizing again. His stance required fewer corrections. His breathing aligned more closely with natural rhythm.

The space no longer resisted every transition.

Søren lowered the device slightly, maintaining the state.

This was not a reversal.

He could not return the system to its prior state.

The initial constraint remained.

Accumulation had occurred.

Paths had been removed.

But...

the system no longer enforced retention.

It was a reintroduction.

A restoration of capacity.

The system did not return to what it had been.

But it changed how it continued.

He could not undo what he had done.

But he could change how it continued.

Future interaction would not begin from the same condition.

The system would not allow unrestricted precision.

Nor unbounded accumulation.

It would require balance.

Whether it was understood or not.

He stepped back.

The movement completed more cleanly now. The delay remained—but softened, less pronounced.

The convergence remained.

But less dense.

Less strained.

The overlapping states still existed—but no longer pressed against one another with the same intensity.

The system held...
with space.

Not empty space.

Available space.

Capacity restored—not by removal—

but by allowing passage.

Søren closed the briefcase.

The latch sealed.

The sound completed fully—no delay.

He stood for a moment, evaluating.

The layers still existed.

The preserved states remained.

But now...
they could pass.

The system no longer refused release.

It permitted it. He turned. The city extended before him. Still aligned. Still precise.

But no longer...
locked.

And as he walked forward, he felt it immediately. His step completed. His breath released. His grip registered at the moment of contact. Not perfect. But possible.

And as he walked forward, one final understanding settled into place:
The first choice had defined the system.
The second—had allowed it to breathe.
It would not prevent what came next.
But it would ensure—it could not begin the same way again.

He took a logn slow deep breath. Then let it out slowly.

Constraint change happened, it almost wasn't possible. These would define future travelers.

He closed his eyes for a moment. He had caused the tightening—and later modified the constraints that followed.

He was successful to reintroduce tolerance from rigid precision to adaptive variation. Restore release mechanism so that states can now resolve and pass. Change constraint behavior from hard constraint that is locked, to soft constraint as adaptive boundary.

He had learn to use it to: reduce precision, increase tolerance, allow release, and change system behavior.

He changed how the system responds to interaction.

He was relaxed, the briefcase secure, the device active, aligned, responsive, it reacts to system pressure, its geometry changes in response to his interaction. This changed how he interacts with the device.

The device had evolved from a tool used as an access mechanism and control interface; to a constraint mediator that translates human intent to system behavior and reflects system pressure to user feedback.

The device was now used not as a machine but a bridge between human intent and system constraint. The constraints could now help future time travelers.

Some had built the device; he helped redefined how it behaves.

Chapter 24: The Living Network

London changed.
Not dramatically. Not visibly.
But fundamentally.

The shift did not announce itself. There was no moment of transition Søren could isolate—no clear boundary where one state ended and another began. It revealed itself gradually, through absence.

The pressure that had defined the city began to ease. Not disappear. Redistribute.

Søren felt it first in his movement. His step completed without the familiar delay. The transfer of weight from one foot to the other settled cleanly, without the subtle correction his body had learned to compensate for. His balance held without adjustment.

His breath followed.

Inhale—complete. Exhale—released. Not held. Not delayed. Continuous.

Søren walked through the city as the system recalibrated—not back to what it had been, but forward into something new.

The layers remained.

But they moved.

The difference was immediate once he allowed himself to see it.

Preserved moments no longer held their positions indefinitely. A hand once suspended completed its gesture. A figure paused mid-step resumed motion and moved forward into the present sequence.

The city no longer carried weight in the same way.

It carried motion. No longer fixed in place. No longer accumulating without release. Circulating. The change was not chaotic. It was measured. Each moment persisted just long enough to maintain continuity, then passed—not erased, not lost, but no longer occupying space within the active structure.

Moments were no longer held indefinitely, but allowed to pass through structure—retained only as long as they remained relevant.

Søren observed the effect at the edge of his vision.

A reflection lingered on glass—then shifted. A fragment of sound extended—then resolved. Nothing rushed. Nothing stalled. The density eased. The strain reduced.

He felt it not as absence—but as freedom of movement. His body no longer adjusted constantly. His stride lengthened slightly. His posture settled into something closer to natural alignment.

Continuity returned. But different. More aware. More deliberate. Not unconscious flow—but structured allowance.

Søren stopped at an intersection and watched.

The pause did not require effort. His body held position without correction, his breathing steady, his perception no longer forced to isolate each interaction.

A preserved gesture—once held—now completed. A hand that had remained extended lowered. A step resumed. A foot that had hovered found the ground and continued forward. A motion finished. Each action resolved not abruptly, but naturally, as though the system had reintroduced timing as a function—not a constraint.

The system was not discarding. It was integrating.

Nothing had been removed. The preserved states remained—but no longer demanded space within the present. That distinction held.

Nothing was lost. Nothing was forced to remain. Everything moved. Søren nodded once. The motion completed fully, without delay.

This was stability. Not a return. A new condition. The system no longer required perfect alignment—only sustainable resolution.

Not through control. Through balance. The distinction settled into him with clarity. Control had required enforcement. Balance allowed continuity to sustain itself.

He moved again.

The city responded—not by adjusting around him, but by including him within its flow.

This difference was subtle—but absolute.

Previously, the system had recognized him as a point of interaction, recalibrating around his presence. Now, his movement required no accommodation. He was not separate from the system.

He was within it. He was no longer a point of interaction. He was part of the system. And the system no longer adjusted for him. It required alignment—but did not enforce it. That had changed.

His steps aligned naturally with the movement around him—not because the system forced it, but because alignment no longer required enforcement.

He reached the embankment. The Thames moved steadily below, its surface reflecting the city above. The reflections behaved differently now. They held—just long enough to confirm structure. Then released. Light traced across the water, lingering at the edges of motion before dissolving into fluid continuity.

Perfect. Not rigid. Not loose. Aligned. Alive.

Søren rested his hand on the railing. The contact registered immediately. He felt the solidity of the metal, the slight coolness against his skin, the stability of the structure beneath him.

But more than that...

he felt the system. Not externally, not as something he observed—internally. His breathing, his balance, his perception—all aligned within the same condition. No separation between observer and structure.

It was no longer forcing precision. It was managing it. Allowing variation within structure. Retaining what mattered. Releasing what did not.

The system no longer held every moment. It selected. Not by force. By relevance. A network. Not a sequence.

Sequences could be followed.

Networks had to be navigated.

That difference would matter...

for anyone who came after.

He was aware of the difference immediately. A sequence required strict progression—one moment leading to the next without deviation.

A network allowed connection, interaction, flow. Moments did not replace one another. They informed one another. He lifted the briefcase slightly and felt its weight.

Changed. Not heavier. Not lighter. Integrated.

The weight no longer stood apart from the system. It belonged within it, subject to the same balance—held when needed, released when not.

The device inside no longer pressed outward as a point of definition.

It no longer defined the system.

It responded to it.

And in doing so...

it limited what could be forced again.

The system would hold.

But not indefinitely.

Not without consequence.

Balance required maintenance...

whether understood or not.

It settled. Part of the structure it had altered. He turned and looked out across the city. London held. Not as a fixed system. But as a living one. Movement flowed. Light shifted. Sound carried and resolved. Nothing forced. Nothing lost.

Everything—allowed.

Chapter 25: The One Who Remains

He returned to the courtyard.
Not because he needed to—but because something in him required confirmation.

The movement back through the city felt different now. His steps completed cleanly. His balance required no correction. The subtle delays that had once defined every transition were gone—or reduced to something natural, no longer structural.

And yet...

he remained aware of them. Not as presence. As memory. The system moved around him—fluid, responsive, balanced. Moments formed, resolved, and passed without accumulation. Nothing pressed. Nothing held beyond its relevance.

Still...

he turned toward the courtyard. The space remained clear. Singular. Unlayered. The transition registered immediately as he entered.

The movement of the city did not follow him inside. The circulating flow—the quiet adaptation—stopped at the threshold. Not abruptly, but completely.

Inside, nothing continued. Everything simply was.

Søren felt the difference in his body again—not as relief this time, but as contrast. His breath moved easily, but without the subtle responsiveness he had begun to recognize outside. His steps settled, but did not carry forward in the same way.

The space did not adapt. It held.

The man stood where he had been before. Unchanged. Not still in the way of pause—but still in the way of completion.

There was no sense of suspension here. No delay. No continuation waiting to occur. The man did not appear preserved.

He appeared finished. Søren approached and stopped.

The distance between them required no adjustment. No alignment. No correction. It simply existed, stable and unchanging.

For a moment, he said nothing. Because the difference between them was no longer conceptual.

It was absolute.

Outside, Søren had become part of a system that moved, adapted, selected, and released.

Here...

none of that applied.

"You adjusted it," the man said.

His voice carried without movement around it—no subtle integration, no variation. It did not pass through the system.

It existed within itself.

Søren nodded. "Yes."

"Not back."

"No."

The man studied him—not with curiosity, but with recognition already settled.

There was no need for interpretation. No evaluation.

Only acknowledgment.

"Forward," he said.

Søren gave the faintest acknowledgment.

"Yes."

Silence followed.

Not held.

Not extended.

Simply present.

The courtyard held its singular continuity, while beyond it the city moved—balanced now, stable, alive.

Søren could sense it even here—not as pressure, but as distant motion. The system continued without him, integrating, adapting, maintaining balance across countless interactions.

Here, nothing advanced.

Nothing accumulated.

Nothing needed to resolve.

Out there...

everything did.

"You understand now," the man said.

Søren did not answer immediately.

Because understanding, now, carried consequence.

It was no longer a matter of perception or control.

It was a condition he existed within.

Then... "Yes."

The word settled fully.

No delay.

No hesitation.

The man nodded once.

"Good."

Søren looked at him more closely.

Not for identity.

For condition.

The man's presence did not shift under observation. There was no variation in posture, no subtle adjustment in stance, no micro-correction of balance. His breathing was present—but not adaptive. It did not respond to the environment.

It completed.

"You're still staying."

"Yes."

"Why?"

The man considered—not searching, but translating something already fixed.

There was no delay in his response—only a measured transition from thought to speech that did not depend on external condition.

Then...

"Because someone has to remember what it was without intervention."

"And what happens without constraint," he continued.

Søren did not respond.

"Before selection became necessary."

Søren held his gaze.

The weight of that no longer felt abstract.

Outside, memory had become integrated—retained only as long as it served the system's balance. Here, memory existed differently.

Not as function.

As boundary.

"A reference," Søren said.

The man inclined his head slightly.

"Not for the system," he said. "For those within it."

Søren understood.

Not structure.

Not memory as data.

Memory as limit.

A point that did not move.

Not to resist change.

But to define it.

"You won't be part of it," Søren said.

"I already am," the man replied. "Just not moving."

Søren's gaze did not shift.

Because now he understood what that meant.

Not moving forward.

Not adapting.

Not changing.

Not continuing.

The man was not waiting.

He was remaining.

Søren exhaled slowly.

The breath completed fully, but without the subtle responsiveness he had begun to associate with the system outside. Here, even that remained singular—contained within itself.

The boundary of the courtyard became clear—not physical, not enforced.

A condition held in place by choice.

And that choice...

did not extend.

It did not propagate.

It did not adapt.

It simply remained what it was.

Then Søren turned.

The motion carried differently here—clean, but without integration. His movement did not influence the space. It did not become part of anything beyond itself.

The courtyard remained. Outside accumulation. Outside adaptation. Outside progression. The man remained. Not left behind. Not preserved. Complete.

"You changed what continues," the man said.

A pause.

"But not what was."

That distinction remained.

Søren stepped toward the threshold.

And as he crossed it...

the difference returned immediately.

The city's motion re-engaged around him. His step aligned within it. His breath resumed its subtle responsiveness. The system included him again... not as an observer, but as participant.

And Søren walked back into the city.

Not as an observer.

Not as an external force.

But as something that continued.

Chapter 26: The Recurrence Ends

He returned to Trafalgar Square at dawn.
Not because it was required...
because something in the system still drew a line back to where it had once tightened.

The movement through the city to reach it felt effortless now—not in the sense of ease, but in the absence of resistance. His steps completed without delay. His balance required no correction. Each shift of weight carried forward into the next without interruption.

And yet...

he remained aware of what had been.

Not as strain. As reference. The square held. Open. Centered. Geometric. But no longer rigid.

The structure remained intact—the symmetry, the lines, the defined relationships between space and form—but the tension that had once held it in exactness had softened. The geometry was still present, but no longer enforced.

It existed because it fit.

The first light of morning moved across the stone in slow gradients, catching edges, softening angles. The fountains cycled—not in perfect repetition, but in measured variation, each arc resolving cleanly before the next began.

The water did not repeat exactly.

It responded.

Each rise and fall completed fully, then gave way to the next—not identical, but aligned.

Nothing forced. Nothing held longer than it should.

Søren stepped into the center.

His shoes met the stone with a quiet finality that did not echo.

The contact registered immediately—no delay, no secondary correction. The sound existed once, completed, and passed.

He stopped.

Waited.

The stillness did not isolate him from the space—it placed him within it. His posture settled without adjustment. His breathing aligned naturally—inhale and exhale completing within the same continuous flow.

There was nothing to correct.

Around him, the city began to move.

A pedestrian crossed the edge of the square—pace natural, uncalculated. Their stride carried forward without interruption, each step resolving cleanly into the next.

A vehicle slowed at the perimeter—not precisely, not mechanically—just enough. The adjustment emerged from context, not enforcement.

A bird lifted, circled, and settled again.

Its motion traced a path that was not pre-defined, but still resolved without deviation. Each movement completed fully before the next began—not because it had to, but because it could.

No duplication. No delay. No correction. Continuity.

Søren remained still.

Not expecting something to appear...
but allowing for the possibility.

The difference mattered. Expectation implied need. Allowance required none.

Nothing did. No figures resolving into place. No second sequence. No residual echo of what had once occupied this point.

The space held only what was present.

Søren let his awareness expand slightly—not searching, but registering. The system did not respond to his attention. It did not tighten. It did not adjust.

It continued.

He shifted his weight slightly.

Even that—carried forward without resistance.

The movement completed without delay. His balance settled naturally, without the need for correction or recalibration.

Because there was nothing left to resolve.

Nothing immediate. Nothing forced. But not nothing.

The realization did not arrive as conclusion.

It was already present in every completed action.

He lifted the briefcase.

Opened it.

The motion was simple now. No lag between intention and contact. The latch released, the lid lifted, each step of the action completing fully before the next began.

The device inside remained stable.

Its internal geometry no longer shifting, no longer adapting, no longer searching.

Søren watched it closely. There was no pulse. No subtle resistance. No need to compensate. It had stopped moving. Not because it was inactive... because it had nothing left to respond to. The system no longer required definition. It no longer required correction. It functioned.

Søren held the moment slightly longer—not out of hesitation, but acknowledgment. The device had not been removed from the system.

It had been absorbed into it.

No longer a point of control. No longer a point of change. Part of what continued.

Søren watched it for a moment longer.

Then closed the case. The latch sealed with a soft, contained finality. The sound completed once. Did not repeat. Did not linger.

A breeze moved through the square.

It passed across the surface of the stone, through the water, along the edges of structure—interacting without altering the system's balance.

Light shifted again—reflections adjusting across the wet stone near the fountains.

For a brief moment, the surface held an image slightly longer than expected.

Søren saw it clearly. The reflection did not distort. Did not duplicate.

It remained...

just past the point where it should have moved.

Not a failure.

Not a break.

Just...

a persistence.

Then it released. The light moved. The surface returned to motion.

Søren noticed. Did not react. His body remained aligned. His breath steady. No correction required. No intervention necessary.

But he did not dismiss it.

Because the system did not eliminate variation.

It allowed it. Within limit. Within balance.

He stood there a moment longer.

Not confirming the system...
but recognizing that completion did not mean absence.

Only balance. That distinction held. Not everything needed to pass immediately. Not everything needed to resolve perfectly.

Only enough...

to continue.

Then he turned.

The motion carried forward without interruption. His body moved naturally into the next step, the next moment, without resistance or delay.

And walked. Not toward another point. Not toward another descent.

Forward.

The direction no longer required definition. It existed because movement continued.

The system did not follow. Did not guide. Did not test.

There was no pressure at his back. No alignment pulling him forward.

It did not need to.

What had ended was not recurrence—but repetition without change. That would not return.

It continued.

Behind him, the square remained—stable, aligned, alive. But not closed. The space did not seal itself into completion.

It remained open to continuation. To variation.

To the possibility of difference within structure.

And as Søren Vahl disappeared into the morning light of London, the city carried on—not repeating, not correcting—

but remembering just enough to continue.

And somewhere within that continuity—

not visible, not disruptive—

something held

for a fraction longer than it should have.

Chapter 27: The Refusal of Time

Time did not stop.
It never had.
What had changed was not time itself—but what was required of it.

Søren walked through the city as it unfolded around him, no longer searching for repetition, no longer testing for error. The movement of things did not resolve into patterns the way he had once expected. It continued—uneven in its details, but stable in its direction.

His steps required no adjustment now. Each movement completed fully, without delay or correction. The subtle resistance that had once separated intention from action was gone. Not removed—no longer necessary.

At the edge of a crossing, a man stepped forward, hesitated for the briefest fraction as a vehicle approached, then continued. The pause was not precise, not calculated. It was small, natural, and unremarkable. The car adjusted in response—not perfectly, not mechanically—but just enough to pass without disruption.

Neither action aligned exactly.
And yet, together, they held.

Søren watched it without intervening. That had been the first change.

Nearby, a conversation carried through the air. Two voices overlapped, one speaker pausing as the other continued, then resuming again without coordination. There was no pattern to it, no enforced rhythm. Nothing repeated.
Nothing needed to.

He no longer measured these moments for deviation. He allowed them to occur as they were—complete in themselves, without requiring correction.

He no longer felt the need to anticipate them either. His breathing moved without interruption, each inhale and exhale completing within the same moment, no longer held between outcomes.

That had been the second change.

He crossed the street.
Waited.
Moved.

The sequence did not resist him. It did not anticipate him. It simply accommodated him, as it did everything else within its range.

By the time he reached the embankment, the city had shifted fully into morning. The open space altered the rhythm behind him—not breaking it, only easing it. The density of movement resolved naturally as the environment allowed it.

He had once mistaken that shift for instability.
It wasn't.
It was capacity.

The Thames moved beside him.

Its surface held the city in fragments of light—lines forming briefly, clear enough to recognize, then dissolving as the current carried them forward.

Each reflection existed just long enough to be part of the whole before releasing itself.

Again.
And again.

He watched longer this time.
Not searching.
Not measuring.
Just seeing.

Two patterns appeared similar—almost identical—then diverged. A slight difference in angle, a shift in brightness, a change in duration too small to isolate but impossible to eliminate.

That was where he had failed before.

He had mistaken consistency for precision.

He had believed that stability required exactness—that time had to align perfectly to remain intact. The system, as he had understood it, was not designed to enforce that kind of order.

It existed to hold variation.
Within limits.

A moment could hesitate.
Adjust.
Shift direction...
and still belong to what came before it.

That was the structure.
Not fixed.
Not repeating.
But continuous.

He rested his hand lightly on the railing. The metal felt solid—not as confirmation, not as validation—just present.

The briefcase sat beside him.
Closed.
Unnecessary.

For a moment, he considered opening it—not out of need, but out of habit. That impulse remained, though weaker now. The need to verify. To confirm. To intervene.

He let the impulse pass.

That was the third change.

Instead, he reached down—not to open the case, but to steady it. His hand rested against the worn surface, feeling the weight settle naturally against the stone.

It was no longer a tool for correction.
But it was not irrelevant.

It had recorded everything.
Not as fixed outcomes—but as boundaries.
Thresholds.
Limits within which variation could occur without collapse.

He understood, then, what could be carried forward.

Not instructions.
Not exact sequences.
But constraints.

Boundaries that allowed variation—without allowing collapse.

The system could not—and should not—be forced into precision. But it could be guided away from failure.

Future travelers would not need to repeat his path.
They would not need to control it.
Only to recognize when control would break it.

They would need to recognize the difference:
Where to allow variation.
Where to prevent collapse.
Where to intervene...
and where not to.

That knowledge could be held.
Not imposed.

He had not learned how to direct time.
He had learned where not to interfere.

He left the case closed.

That was the fourth change.

The river continued.
The city continued.

And he continued with them—not separate, not controlling, not correcting, but present within the same movement.

For a moment, something held.

A reflection lingered just slightly longer than it should have—not enough to disrupt, not enough to define—but enough to be noticed.

Søren saw it.
Did not move.

The reflection released.

Nothing broke.
Nothing corrected it.
Nothing erased it.

That was the final confirmation.

The system did not require perfection.
It required tolerance.

He lifted the briefcase and let it settle naturally into his hand. Its weight no longer pulled against him. It moved with him.

Integrated.

The weight aligned with his movement without resistance, no longer something he carried against the system, but within it.

He turned from the railing.

The city extended ahead—unresolved, unstructured, and entirely intact.

He walked.

Not toward a destination.
Not toward a convergence.

What he had changed would not prevent what came next—only ensure it could not begin the same way again.

But forward...
within a continuity that did not need to repeat to remain whole.

And as Søren Vahl disappeared into the living movement of the city, one truth remained—not stated, not imposed, but carried forward in every uncorrected moment.

Time had not been controlled.
It had not been corrected.
It had been refused...
only in the ways it demanded to be fixed.

And in that refusal...
it had finally been allowed to continue.

Epilogue: The City That Continues

London remained. Not unchanged. Not perfected.
Alive.

The city did not return to what it had been. It continued from what it had become—carrying forward variation without forcing it into uniformity, holding structure without fixing it in place.

Morning moved through the streets in measured variation—footsteps overlapping, separating, continuing. A door closed. A voice carried, paused, resumed. Light shifted across glass and stone, holding briefly before passing on.

Sound no longer arranged itself into clean sequence. It layered, separated, rejoined—each moment completing without needing to align perfectly with the next.

Nothing repeated.
Nothing was forced to resolve beyond what it could hold.

The system remained.
Not imposed.
Not withdrawn.
Present.

It no longer pressed against movement or required confirmation. It existed within it—quietly maintaining the conditions that allowed continuity without enforcing it.

Moments flowed.

Most passed cleanly.

Some lingered—just long enough to be noticed.

A hesitation at a crossing.

A pedestrian stepping forward, pausing not out of calculation, but instinct, then continuing without disruption.

A reflection that held a fraction longer than expected before dissolving into motion.

Light tracing across glass, lingering at an angle just beyond expectation—then releasing without resistance.

A gesture that seemed, for an instant, to echo itself...
then completed.

Not errors.

Reminders.

Of what had once been held too tightly.
And what had been allowed to pass.

At the edge of the city, in a narrow courtyard between buildings, the space remained singular.

Clear.
Unlayered.

The transition into it still marked a difference—not abrupt, not enforced, but complete. The movement of the city did not follow. It did not need to.

The man still stood there.

Not waiting.
Not observing in the way others did.
Remaining.

His presence did not shift with time. It did not adapt, did not integrate, did not participate in the system's balance.

It held.

Not as resistance.

As completion.

His presence did not influence the system.
It did not need to.

It marked something the system itself no longer contained.

A reference.

For what had existed before choice became visible.

Beyond the courtyard, the city continued.

Balanced.
Adaptive.
Unfinished.

Movement carried forward without repetition. Variation persisted within limits. Nothing required exactness to remain intact.

And somewhere within that continuity—unseen, unmarked—the structure still existed.

Not as a point of control.
Not as something to return to.
But as something that could be reached.

What he lived was not removal but redistribution, not control but balance, not precision but permission.

The consequence was that system still requires: maintenance, understanding, and participation.

The future system is now navigable, not controllable.

Future users would inherit constraints and interpret differently.

Not through necessity.
Through decision.

A moment.
A condition.
A possibility.

It did not call. It did not guide. It did not impose itself on those who moved within the system.

It remained available.

Waiting...
not for correction...
but for recognition.

Again.
And always.

Not all travelers arrive at the same moment.
And not all of them leave.

Appendix A: Principles of Continuity and Alignment

A Note to the Reader

What follows is not a complete system. It is an observed one.

These principles were not given, taught, or designed to be understood in isolation. They were encountered—piece by piece—through interaction, consequence, and constraint.

They do not explain the system.They describe how it behaves.

---

1. Continuity Is Maintained

Continuity is not automat ic.

It is sustained through alignment.

Events do not proceed simply because time moves forward. They proceed because the system allows them to resolve.

---

2. Alignment Is Permission

Alignment does not mean something is correct.

It means something is allowed to hold.

A moment may be aligned without being complete, optimal, or final.

---

3. Constraint Defines Stability

Constraint is not restriction.

It is structure.

It determines what can exist without collapsing into conflict.

Without constraint, all states compete for the same space.

---

4. Tolerance Enables Continuity

Tolerance allows variation.

It permits imperfection, delay, and human inconsistency.

Without tolerance, every deviation must either resolve immediately—or remain.

---

5. Precision Reduces Tolerance

Precision strengthens alignment.

But it narrows possibility.

As precision increases, the system becomes less able to absorb variation.

Stability improves.

Adaptability declines.

---

6. The System Preserves

The system does not correct what has occurred.

It retains it.

Even incomplete or imperfect states persist unless explicitly released.

---

7. Partial States Continue

No action is neutral.

Incomplete alignment does not disappear.

It carries forward, influencing all subsequent structure.

---

8. Duplication Is Conflict

Duplication occurs when two states occupy the same space.

It creates structural instability.

It cannot be sustained.

---

9. Echo Is Persistence

Echo is not duplication.

It is a moment that exists twice in time, not space.

It is a residue of what has not yet been released.

---

10. Resolution Is Completion

Some elements do not persist.

They resolve.

They exist only long enough to complete a transition.

Not everything is meant to remain.

---

11. The System Selects

The system is not passive.

It places, aligns, and removes based on structural need.

What appears is not random.

It is required.

---

12. Depth Is Not Direction

Terms like *below* or *inside* do not indicate location.

They indicate structure.

They refer to levels where alignment is no longer surface-based.

---

13. Nodes Define Change

Not all locations are equal.

Certain points allow structural change.

At these points, alignment becomes decision.

---

14. The System Responds to Interaction

Observation changes nothing.

Interaction does.

The system adapts to engagement, not awareness.

---

15. Failure Is Indecision

The system does not fail through collapse.

It fails when it cannot determine what to release.

At that point, everything remains.

---

16. Accumulation Is Pressure

When moments are not released, they accumulate.

This does not break the system immediately.

It compresses it.

---

17. Balance Requires Release

Stability is not achieved through control alone.

It requires the ability to let moments pass.

Retention without release leads to saturation.

---

18. Continuity Is Adaptive

The system is not fixed.

It adjusts.

Not by removing structure, but by rebalancing it.

---

19. Completion Is Not Finality

Resolution does not end the system.

It changes its behavior.

Even in stability, variation remains.

---

20. The System Remains Open

The system is never fully closed.

Possibility persists.

Not as error.

But as potential.

Final Observation

Time is not something that moves independently.

It is something that is continuously shaped by what is allowed to remain—

and what is allowed to pass.

About the Author

Mark Anderson, PhD, writes at the intersection of artificial intelligence, human decision-making, and complex systems. His work explores how intelligent systems interact with human judgment—especially in environments where precision, risk, and uncertainty must coexist.-

Blending technical depth with philosophical insight, he examines not only how systems function, but how decisions emerge within them—where time, perception, reality, and stability were never about control.

Style Notes

This book is written a little differently—on purpose.

You may notice short lines.
Intentional pauses.
Moments that feel incomplete or unresolved.

Some thoughts trail off… suggesting uncertainty or hesitation.
Some break apart—shifting meaning mid-sentence.
Others move more fluidly, carrying ideas forward with a quieter rhythm.

At times, punctuation is used more expressively than traditionally:
—dashes are used to shift or interrupt a thought or sequence
… ellipses to suggest hesitation or uncertainty
, commas to soften the flow of a sentence

White space is part of the experience.
It allows room for reflection—for the moment between understanding and choice. The differences should "feel" real in your mind as you read.

These are not formatting mistakes.
They are part of how the story is meant to be read.

Some scenes are meant to land quickly.
Others are meant to linger.

If you find yourself slowing down, rereading a sentence, or pausing between paragraphs,
the book is working exactly as intended.

That quiet moment of awareness—the instant you step back and observe your own thinking—
is where the most important conversations in this story truly begin.

This is a story meant to be experienced as much as it is read.

"The structure uses intentional pacing, fragmentation, and punctuation to reflect uncertainty, decision-making, and perception in time."

Description:

Søren Vahl encounters a system that does not manipulate time but aligns it—structuring moments into precise continuity where nothing is left unresolved. At first, the effect appears to create perfect stability: actions complete cleanly, outcomes align, and variation is reduced.

However, as the system tightens, unintended consequences emerge. Moments no longer pass freely. Events begin to accumulate rather than resolve. Time does not collapse—it becomes increasingly constrained, holding more than it can release.

As the structure evolves, Søren is forced to reconsider the nature of stability itself. What begins as an attempt to eliminate instability becomes a deeper exploration of how systems maintain continuity—not through precision, but through tolerance, variation, and selective release.

Through a series of increasingly complex interactions, Søren moves from control to recognition, discovering that time does not require correction, but balance within defined limits.

This philosophical science fiction novel examines:

- time as a dynamic system rather than a fixed sequence
- the relationship between precision and stability
- the role of variation, constraint, and release in complex systems
- the limits of control in human and artificial structures

The London Recurrence is a contemplative work of speculative fiction that explores time, perception, and continuity through a systems-based lens, offering a unique perspective on how order emerges without enforcement.

Back Cover

THE LONDON RECURRENCE

The Refusal of Time

Time was never broken. It was held too tightly.

When Søren Vahl discovers a system capable of aligning time itself, he does what anyone would do—he perfects it.

Moments resolve exactly. Movement aligns precisely. Nothing is left to chance. And slowly—almost invisibly—everything begins to fail. Not through collapse. Through accumulation. Moments stop passing. Choices stop releasing. Time begins to remember too much.

As the world tightens around him, Søren is forced to confront a deeper truth: stability does not come from precision—it comes from allowing what cannot be controlled.

What follows is not a race to fix time, but a journey to understand it. Not how to control it. But where not to. He doesn't write instructions. He creates conditions that must be followed. He can alter how the device interacts with the system.

A philosophical science fiction novel about time, choice, and the limits of control.

Also by Mark Anderson

- *The Meridian Paris Protocol – Book 1 of the Meridian series*
- *The London Recurrence – Book 2 of the Meridian series*
- *The Alignment Echo (Books I, II, III) - SciFi*
- *Does AI Scare You? Yes. No. Maybe.*
- *Tommi the Green Tomato (Bilingual Series)*
- *Finnish with Purpose*
- *Swedish and Portuguese with Purpose - Coming Soon*
- *The Accidental Genius & Snackcidents (Cookbook)*
- *Cooking and Cancer (Cooking for someone special)*

The Meridian Series

Where time is not fixed—and neither is choice.

Book 1: *The Meridian Paris Protocol*

Things are Not What They Remember

The system is discovered.

A solitary traveler arrives in Paris and uncovers a hidden structure designed to stabilize time itself.
But stability demands a single outcome—and the cost of removing uncertainty may be everything.

Book 2: *The London Recurrence*
The Refusal of Time

The system resists control.

As intervention replaces observation, the system begins to react—repeating, correcting, and narrowing possibility.
Control becomes consequence, and precision reveals its limits.

Book 3: *The Tokyo Convergence*

Coming Soon

The system becomes something else.

In Tokyo, the boundaries between observer and system collapse.
Multiple paths intersect, and a new form of time begins to emerge—one that cannot be contained, predicted, or undone.

www.ingramcontent.com/pod-product-compliance
Lightning Source LLC
LaVergne TN
LVHW010651110826
845149LV00014B/3030

* 9 7 9 8 9 9 5 8 0 8 5 8 9 *